"There's Only One Pillow,"
He Told Jessie.

Crouching inside the covered back of the pickup truck, Hank spread out the sleeping bag. They had both gotten wet from the rain. "Get under the blanket," he told her. Shivering, Jessie was glad to comply. He nestled her up against him with his arms around her.

She moved a little, snuggling closer. Instant desire flared in his body. "Lie still," he growled.

"Sorry," she said.

His voice became cynical. "I'll just bet you are."

He was aroused and angry about it, Jessie suspected. "Don't be mad," she whispered. "Hank, the only time I feel safe is when I'm with you."

"Go to sleep."

"Do you remember the first time we made love?"

"Jessie, for God's sake...."

Smiling, Jessie curved one arm under her head and slipped the other around his waist. It landed just below his belt buckle.

"Be sure you know what you're doing," he cautioned.

Dear Reader:

Welcome to Silhouette Desire! If you're a regular reader, you already know you're in for a treat. If this is your first Silhouette Desire, I predict you'll be hooked on romance, because these are sensuous, emotional love stories written by and for today's women—women just like *you!*

A Silhouette Desire can have many different moods and tones: some are humorous, others dramatic. But they *all* have a heroine you can identify with. She's busy, smart, and occasionally downright frazzled! She's always got something keeping her on the go: family, sometimes kids, maybe a job and there's that darned car that keeps breaking down! And of course, she's got that extra complication—the sexy, interesting man she's just met....

Speaking of sexy men, don't miss May's *Man of the Month* title, *Sweet on Jessie,* by Jackie Merritt. This man is just wonderful. Also, look for *Just Say Yes,* another terrific romance from the pen of Dixie Browning. Rounding out May are books by Lass Small, Rita Rainville, Cait London and Christine Rimmer. It's a great lineup, and naturally I hope you read them all.

So, until next month, happy reading!

Lucia Macro
Senior Editor

JACKIE MERRITT

SWEET ON JESSIE

SILHOUETTE *Desire*®

Published by Silhouette Books New York

America's Publisher of Contemporary Romance

SILHOUETTE BOOKS
300 East 42nd St., New York, N.Y. 10017

SWEET ON JESSIE

ISBN: 0-373-05642-7

First Silhouette Books printing May 1991

Printed in the U.S.A.

Books by Jackie Merritt

Silhouette Desire

JACKIE MERRITT

and her husband live just outside of Las Vegas, Nevada. An accountant for many years, Jackie has happily traded numbers for words. Next to family, books are her greatest joy, both for reading and writing.

One

Hank Farrell stood at the counter of Fisher's Convenience Store, holding a six-pack of beer and a gallon of milk. One customer, elderly Pete Hogan, was ahead of him and in the middle of telling a long story to Lois Fisher, who was behind the counter. Lois shot Hank an apologetic look and attempted to urge Pete along. Hank grinned and shrugged. Everyone in Thorp, Wyoming, liked Pete, but he was notoriously long-winded.

Several other customers were in the small store, and Hank knew them all. There were few strangers in Thorp. Located in long-established ranching country, the little town's merchants did a thriving business. Its bank was busy, it had two elementary schools, an impressive new high school, a small hospital and a decent library.

Hank shifted his weight from one dusty boot to the other. He'd walked miles that day and was dirty and sweaty. If Pete ever got through with his story, Hank intended to pay for his milk and beer and head for home and a quiet evening.

Then, from one of the aisles, snatches of a conversation between two young women, Kelly Travers and Cindy Miller, reached Hank's ears.

"I heard that she's going to be here all summer."

"Well, with poor Ann having to stay in bed until September, Jessie will certainly be a help. Of course, Bob and Ann have Mavis, but there's really no substitute for family during a crisis, is there?"

Jessie . . . Ann . . . Bob . . . Mavis? Hank's ears pricked up while his pulse went crazy.

"Imagine Jessie being away from her husband all summer, though. Don't you find that a little strange?"

"Not necessarily, Kelly. Jessie and Bob were always very close, you know."

The conversation would have meant nothing to anyone unaware of Thorp's citizenry. But Hank knew very well that Jessie and Bob Shroeder were sister and brother, and that Ann was Bob's wife. Mavis was their housekeeper. He'd also heard, through the years, that Ann had suffered several miscarriages. She was pregnant again, and it was only logical to conclude, from this conversation, that her doctor had demanded bed rest in hope of forestalling another miscarriage.

While all of that was a part of Thorp and only common knowledge, one part of Cindy's and Kelly's little chat nearly struck Hank dumb. Jessie was here, in Thorp, for the summer. He concentrated on the two voices behind him, but the women had switched topics.

"Hank?"

Blinking, Hank realized that Pete had finally left and Lois was ready to wait on him. He suddenly felt clumsy and it seemed to be an awkward chore to dig out his wallet. Even his mouth felt numb, and he could hardly answer Lois's friendly comments. When he'd paid and received his change, he walked away from the counter and was almost to the door when Lois laughed. "Aren't you going to take these things you just bought, Hank?"

Mumbling something unintelligible, Hank returned to the counter, grabbed his milk and beer and hurried out of the store. He got into his pickup, then sat there woodenly. Jessie Shroeder was back. He couldn't seem to think beyond that point. *Jessie was back!*

"Anything wrong, Hank?"

Hank's dazed eyes moved to the open window. Cindy Miller was looking at him curiously. Instantly, an overwhelming urge to ask Cindy exactly what she knew about Jessie shook Hank, and it was all he could do to suppress it. "No, nothing's wrong, Cindy. Thanks for asking."

Cindy smiled. "Well, you were just sitting there. I thought maybe your truck wouldn't start."

"It's fine." Hank turned the ignition key. With a small wave, he backed the pickup out of the parking space, then drove out onto the street.

The Farrell ranch was two miles outside of Thorp. Hank made it home on pure instinct. When he pulled up and stopped the pickup next to his house, he turned off the engine and just sat again. He'd spent eight years—hell, longer than that—trying to get Jessie Shroeder out of his system. He'd thought, he'd *hoped,* that he'd succeeded.

Hank shook his head, as if to clear it. Just hearing Jessie's name had brought back a ton of ambiguous memories. She'd married another man. She'd chosen a fancy-pants rich guy from California over him. What was her married name? Oh, yes, Vaughn. She'd married Allen Vaughn.

The past buffeted Hank, years stacking one on another, specific events he'd tried to bury and forget. It was all there, who he'd been, who Jessie had been. Regret mingled with resentment. The regret was his own and deeply felt; the resentment was for whom? Jessie? The town? He knew he'd been wild as a teenager, breaking every rule, defying his own parents and even the law. With Jessie, though, he'd been different—tender, gentle and deeply in love.

But Jessie had married someone else.

Feeling again the agony of betrayal, the same chaotic frustration he'd suffered eight years ago, Hank slapped the steering wheel in anger, then climbed out of the truck and carried his purchases into the house. Maybe he had no one to blame but himself for the past, although he knew his anger was directed at Jessie. She had allowed her family and the town's attitude toward "that wild Farrell boy" to come between them.

Even though she had loved him. That's what nearly killed Hank every time he thought about it. Jessie had loved *him!* He was positive of it.

Hank stood at the kitchen sink and broodingly stared out the window. The Farrell place had changed a lot in the past few years. Hank's father had raised a common breed of cattle and had nearly starved doing it. After his parents' deaths, Hank had tried to come up with something more to do with the ranch he'd inherited and ultimately had branched out into Appaloosa horses, rodeo bulls and German shepherd dogs.

Another sideline was a helicopter charter service. Hank owned a four-seater helicopter and earned very good money doing something he also loved, flying. The ranch made a good profit now. There were still remnants of the wild youth he'd been in the man he was today, but Hank Farrell was a pretty solid citizen these days.

He'd never married. He'd never found anyone he could love the way he had loved Jessie.

Wearily rubbing the back of his neck, Hank got one of the cans of beer he'd brought home. The back door of the house opened. "Hank?"

"In the kitchen." Mick O'Dwyer, Hank's one employee, came in. "Want a beer?"

"Sure, thanks. A cold beer would taste good." Mick took the beer Hank handed him, popped the top and took a long swallow. "I just stopped in to tell you that the dogs have been fed and watered, and everything's done for the day."

"Thanks, Mick."

Mick was a smallish man, only a little older than Hank, with piercing black eyes. They narrowed on Hank. "You look like hell. Something wrong?"

"Just tired, I guess." He had good reason for being tired. He'd tramped over five hundred acres that day, speculating all the while about the land's investment potential. Hank only maintained a moderate bank balance, preferring to invest extra cash in local real estate. In a small way, he was becoming something of an entrepreneur. The classy word made Hank laugh when he thought of it. He wasn't trying to amass any kind of fortune. Everything he did was to keep busy. The dogs, the horses, the bulls and the flying service kept him on his toes most of the time, which was the way Hank liked it.

But Mick knew him better than most people did. As a lifelong friend and cohort in some of the more daring escapades of Hank's youth, Mick wasn't one to be put off by such an evasive remark. Hank could tell by the look on the smaller man's face that he suspected more than simple tiredness was causing the strain in his old friend's eyes.

Was there any point to evasion? Hank asked himself. Mick knew most of what had occurred in the past, and it would only be a matter of time until he heard about Jessie's return to Thorp. Mick had been there, a friend when Hank had badly needed a friend. "Jessie's in town," he said with a bluntness that conveyed some of the emotional upheaval he was undergoing.

Mick didn't say anything right away, but Hank could see him digesting the information. Finally, after another swig from his can of beer, Mick asked, "Have you seen her?"

"I only just heard about it. Kelly Travers and Cindy Miller were discussing it in Fisher's when I stopped for a few things." Hank felt another question in the air, but he knew Mick wouldn't ask it: Are you *going* to see her?

Hank had no ready answer to that question anyway, even if Mick had spelled it out in a dozen different ways. See Jessie, as in deliberately seeking her out? An accidental meeting was one thing, an intentional contact, quite another. Only a fool would purposely go looking for emotional pain, and, God help him, he wasn't still a fool about Jessie, was he?

Hank stared out the window again. "She's going to be here all summer." He related what Cindy and Kelly had talked about in a flat, toneless voice. Mick listened without comment until Hank brought his gaze from the window.

Then Mick quietly reminded, "She's been back before, Hank."

"Twice," Hank agreed, the set of his lips relaying tension. "For her folks' funerals. Two days out of eight years." His implication hung in the air. Two very brief visits to Thorp couldn't be compared to several months in town. Besides, the funerals had been extremely private affairs, with only family and very close friends in attendance, and Hank certainly hadn't been included. He hadn't so much as gotten a glimpse of Jessie on those two occasions.

He could see that the subject was making Mick uncomfortable. It was making Hank uncomfortable, too, but he had to live with it; Mick didn't. "Forget it, Mick. It will all come out in the wash," he said with a grim smile.

Mick drained his can of beer, and Hank sensed the smaller man's relief. It wasn't that Mick wouldn't talk about anything Hank needed to, but what was there to say about this matter? Jessie was back, and both men knew that Hank was going to be affected by it, in one way or another.

"Well, I better be going," Mick mumbled with apparent uncertainty.

Hank nodded. Mick had a wife and kids to get home to, and his day of work was over. "Right. See you tomorrow."

With Mick gone, Hank finished his beer and went upstairs for a shower. Then, with a towel wrapped around his hips, he went back downstairs, got another beer and went outside. Two years before, he'd built a redwood hot tub on the back patio. It had whirlpool jets and was the one place Hank didn't mind wasting a little time. After removing the cover from the tub and turning on the jets, Hank dropped the towel and climbed into the steaming, bubbling hot water.

The can of cold beer was within reach, and Hank laid his head back and closed his eyes. The hot, moving water felt soothing, as it always did, but behind his eyelids, he saw Jessie.

Eight years. It seemed more like a hundred, and yet, in another way, like only yesterday.

When he'd been seventeen, Jessie had been fourteen. That's when he began noticing her. The Shroeders had been "somebodies" in Thorp. Jessie's father had owned the bank, and her older brother, Bob, was already in college, preparing for law school. Jessie had changed from a gawky little girl into a beautiful young woman overnight, or so it had seemed.

Hank and Jessie had been like day and night, on opposite sides of the proverbial tracks, although the railroad really ran a quarter mile east of town. Jessie was the protected youngest child of a well-to-do family; Hank was the son of a not-very-successful rancher.

Affluence hadn't been the deterrent to social intercourse between the Farrells and the Shroeders, though. Thorp's residents had few pretensions, and during Robert Shroeder's, Jessie's father's, lifetime, one was as likely to see the solemnly dignified man in blue jeans as in a banker's suit. The fact was, Hank had cut his own throat with the Shroeders. He'd known, as surely as he'd known his own name, that they had despised his go-to-hell attitude and reckless plunge through life. And with all of the cocksure confidence he'd possessed then, he'd thought it hadn't mattered.

It *had* mattered. It had mattered enough to Jessie that she had married another man.

Hank reached out with a not quite steady hand for the can of beer and drank half of it. Jessie's long, dark hair and soft brown eyes filled his mind. She'd been so beautiful, so bright and young and alive, that she'd taken his breath away every time he'd seen her.

With his eyes closed again, Hank's thoughts jumped from sporadic, accidental meetings to several years later. He'd been in college for almost three years. At twenty-one, when he came home from Cheyenne in April, Jessie had been finishing her senior year of high school.

He'd had a terrible fight with his dad. "Getting kicked out of college is a disgrace!" the elder Farrell had raged.

Hank had been tired of school and glad to be done with it. "Don't expect me to try another school," he had said coldly. "I'm through with school."

The argument had gone on for several days, until Hank had gotten so tired of it, he'd avoided the house. He didn't know what he wanted to do with his life, he had no plans. But he wasn't afraid of hard work and felt something would turn up.

Hank knew now that he'd attracted every rowdy, careless person in the area back then. His crowd drank too much, got into fist fights, drove recklessly and were generally a bunch of goof-offs. Some of that old group had finally grown up, as he had, and were now an integral part of the same establishment they'd had so much disdain for.

The thing was, Jessie never had been on the outside of the establishment, and she hadn't liked being attracted to a boy with Hank Farrell's reputation.

Taking another swallow of beer, Hank remembered how hard Jessie had fought against liking him. After her high school graduation, he hadn't been able to stay away from her. He'd made up his mind that he wanted Jessie Shroeder, and he had gone after her. Without the least bit of shame or apology, he kept showing up wherever she went. It wasn't at all difficult to keep track of the activities around town, and where Jessie went, so did Hank.

He finally wore her objections down enough that she agreed to a date with him. By the end of that summer, Hank was working for his father on the ranch and seeing Jessie once every week. She couldn't allow more than that, not when her parents and brother were so dead set against her seeing Hank at all.

By Labor Day, Hank was nearly crazy from wanting Jessie. He never got more than one good-night kiss from her after each date, and Jessie was all he thought about. That fall, she went off to college and he suffered agonies until the Christmas holiday.

They had been writing letters back and forth, so Hank knew the exact day Jessie was due home. He phoned the Shroeder house and got the runaround three times, until finally Bob yelled in his ear, "Why in hell don't you take the hint, Farrell? No one in this family wants anything to do with you!"

That had been the most open declaration of hostility Hank had encountered with any of the Shroeders, and it had set the tone of his and Bob Shroeder's relationship, seemingly in concrete. Finishing the last of his beer, Hank thought about how frustrated and powerless Bob had made him feel that day. Bob's dislike had been something to laugh off until then.

The Shroeders were selling their bank to a chain that winter. Robert Shroeder had developed serious heart problems, and Bob was already a practicing attorney. Hank told himself to ignore Bob. The man was a soft-handed, suit-wearing jerk, and while Hank would have liked nothing better than to confront him face-to-face, alienating Jessie's family more than he already had wouldn't help his case any.

During that two-week holiday, he'd seen Jessie exactly once.

Hank's trip into the past was suddenly interrupted by the telephone. He'd installed an outside bell to prevent missing important calls, and he jumped out of the hot tub, grabbed the towel and hurried into the house.

It was Jim Garrison, a real estate agent who often showed potential buyers of large tracts of land how the property looked from the air. Jim made a date to charter the helicopter for the following Saturday morning. When the call was over, Hank decided he'd had enough of hot water and reminiscing. He was over the shock of hearing about Jessie's return, and what good would it do to belabor the past again?

He would have to accept Jessie's proximity for the summer; he had no choice.

Bob and Ann lived in the same house Jessie had grown up in. The large two-story structure was old, but well-cared for and very dear to Jessie. Being home again was unbelievably comforting, almost permitting Jessie to forget the trauma of the past eight years.

Almost, but not quite. Nothing could make her really forget, and as a matter of fact, the counselor she'd been seeing in Los Angeles had impressed upon her that she shouldn't waste time in even trying to forget. "You lived through it, Jessie. It's a part of your life, and we never really forget anything so shattering. What you must concentrate on is a cessation of self-blame. Battered wives often take the blame for their husbands' abuse, and nothing could be further from the truth."

Jessie's mind was full of good advice and intelligent, considerate conversations. Time would be the best healer, she knew, but she also knew the value of talking to a professional.

There was peace here, Jessie thought as she strolled around the immense grounds within the iron fence surrounding the Shroeder home. She felt safe here, although Allen was no longer a threat. Not only were they divorced, Jessie had heard that Allen was undergoing counseling, too. If it were true, she was glad he was getting professional help; she felt that he desperately needed it.

She hadn't seen him in nearly a year, although he had called several times and begged her to meet him somewhere to talk. Jessie suspected that her ex-husband wanted a reconciliation, and the thought was a nightmare. After so many terrible, terrifying years, she looked on the divorce as a release from oppression, and she didn't even want to talk to Allen, let alone see him.

Then, at a very opportune time in her life, Bob had called and talked about Ann's forced bed rest. Jessie had previously told her brother about the divorce, of course, but not about its cause. Allen's family knew about his rages, but Jessie saw no good reason to inform her brother and sister-in-law of her ex-husband's instability. Bob and Ann had their own problems, what with Ann's health and their almost frantic desire to have a child, and besides, despite extensive counseling and common sense to the contrary, Jessie couldn't completely eradicate a sense of shame over living with an abusive husband for almost eight years.

To Jessie, Bob's call had seemed heaven-sent. She had been wanting to get out of L.A. for a while, just until she got her bearings and decided what she wanted to do with the rest of her life. She had suggested spending the summer helping Ann, and Bob had been overjoyed about it. It wasn't a matter of cooking or doing the laundry. Bob and Ann had a very capable housekeeper. But the little extras, maybe just sitting by Ann's bed and keeping her company or doing some shopping for her, were things that Mavis Goodrow just didn't have time for.

Jessie plucked a stalk of tall grass growing at one of the iron fence posts and chewed on it as she walked. Thorp was such a nice little town, and she had returned only twice since her marriage, both sad occasions, the funerals of her parents.

No, she wasn't going to think of that now, Jessie decided. It was a beautiful day and she was going to think of pleasant things, like, how many of her former friends were still living in the area. Smiling softly, Jessie thought of the girls and boys she'd grown up with. There were a few that she would give almost anything to see again.

And then there was Hank Farrell. Did he still live here? Was he married?

Jessie's smile faded as she wondered if she hadn't just landed on another disruptive topic. Hank was such a point of private dissension. She'd thought of him so many, many times, especially when she had realized the dreadful mistake she'd made in marrying Allen.

In retrospect, Jessie knew that she hadn't been very wise with men. But Hank still held a special place in her heart, wise or not. She sighed hopelessly, seeing Hank's image in her mind's eye. His handsome face had radiated his wild streak. His long, tousled black hair and devilish blue eyes had screamed nonconformity. To Hank, nothing had been sacred or off-limits. He'd behaved as though he'd been above the law and even common decency.

And he'd fallen madly in love with her and had nearly convinced her that she loved him, too.

Jessie sighed again. She'd chosen Allen, which proved how little she'd understood men back then. But choosing Hank would have been a mistake, too.

For a moment, a little of Hank's old magic invaded Jessie's system and she stopped in her tracks. His kisses, his caresses...had anything else she'd ever experienced made her feel so...so wanton? So female?

Jessie began walking again. Hank Farrell had been bad news, and while she hadn't been right in marrying Allen, she'd definitely been right in *not* marrying Hank!

No, she did not and would not allow herself to care if Hank still lived in Thorp or if he was married, either. She hadn't come back here to renew that disturbing phase of her life. In fact, at present, the thought of *any* man was actually repellent. It would be a long, long time before she trusted a man again.

For three days Hank functioned on routine and habit. Try as he might, he couldn't forget that Jessie was in Thorp and living in the Shroeders' old mansion on Front Street. He drove by the place one night after dark, then cursed himself for idiocy. Mooning after any married woman was ridiculous; mooning after Jessie, doubly so.

Bob Shroeder still could hardly say a civil hello to him. It was a silly, childish attitude for a seemingly otherwise intelligent adult, but Hank still felt the man's animosity when they ran into each other. Not that their paths crossed all that often. Even in Thorp, as small as it was, there wasn't much reason for a Farrell and a Shroeder to get together. Another attorney, Rich Newfield, had moved to town a few years back, and Hank took his legal business to him. Hank wasn't much for clubs, either, so he wasn't a member of the Elks or the Eagles lodges, places he might have run into Bob.

On Saturday morning, Hank flew Jim Garrison and his client to the Bear Mountain area. The flight took three hours, and when they got back, Hank serviced and washed the helicopter. He did a few chores around the ranch that afternoon, then found himself wandering around like a lost soul.

He knew what his problem was, like it or not: he wanted to see Jessie. He wanted to see her so badly, the feeling was like a fist in his gut. He could tell himself a hundred times a day how stupid deliberately seeking out Jessie would be, but he couldn't stop his feelings. His jaw clenched spasmodically while he fought an internal battle on the matter. Why did he want to see her when just knowing she was in Thorp made his stomach roil with dark emotions? What good would come out of seeing Jessie? What did they have to say to each other, anyway?

It had all been said eight years ago, and now, Jessie was married. She was another man's wife.

But was that what was stopping him? When had he gotten so timid? When had he become so settled and accepting of what other people considered wrong or improper that he stopped himself from doing what *he* wanted?

It would be wiser to stay away from Jessie. Hank knew that with complete certainty, but he was sick and tired of the ache in his gut. All he wanted was to see her, to talk to her a little. Was that really so terrible?

Making up his mind abruptly, Hank strode to the house. He showered, shaved and put on clean clothes. And then he got into his pickup and drove to Thorp.

The entire trip, from his ranch to Front Street, took less than ten minutes. When he saw the Shroeder place, he was tempted to drive on past. But, gritting his teeth, he boldly pulled into the driveway.

Mavis Goodrow answered the door. "Why, Hank Farrell!"

Clearly, Mavis was mystified to see him on the Shroeders' front porch. "Hello, Mavis. I understand Jessie is here."

"Well, yes, she is . . . and she isn't. What I mean is, she's home for the summer, but she isn't here right now. She went down to Cleavers to get something for Ann."

Cleavers was the closest thing to a department store Thorp had. Smack dab in the center of town, Cleavers carried a little of almost anything one might need.

Hank nodded thoughtfully. Confronting Jessie in Cleavers didn't set quite right, but waiting here until she got back didn't, either. And now that he'd come this far, he was determined to at least say hello to Jessie.

"Thanks, Mavis. I'll catch her in town." Hank walked away, fully aware of Mavis's curious stare at his back. If she wasn't remembering him chasing Jessie years ago, he'd be forever surprised, he thought with a taut grimace. He'd accomplished one thing today, even if he didn't find Jessie. It would be all over town tomorrow that he'd appeared on the Shroeders' doorstep and asked for Jessie.

Two

Ann had asked Jessie to go down to Cleavers to buy her some new nightgowns. "Something with high necks and sleeves," Ann had requested with a laugh. "Almost everything I have is a little too revealing for company, and if I have to stay in bed, I want to see everyone who is kind enough to stop by."

Jessie found four nightgowns with Ann's requirements and bought them all. Carrying the package, Jessie browsed through Cleavers. At a rack of blouses, she pulled out a royal-blue one and held it up to examine its design.

"That color is perfect for you."

Everything in Jessie stiffened. Even without looking, she knew who was standing there.

"Hello, Jessie."

She turned slowly. Her heart was pounding loud enough to hear. "My God, you look exactly the same," she exclaimed huskily with her first hasty inspection of Hank Farrell.

She didn't look the same. Hank couldn't believe how much Jessie had changed. She was very thin, and there were dark smudges beneath her eyes. Her high cheekbones were distinctly pronounced, as was the angle of her jaw. Her hair was much shorter than the image he carried around with him, stopping at her jawline. It was curled and stylish, but so very different from the long, loose hair he remembered.

The most startling change was in her eyes. Jessie's expressive brown eyes had always danced, as though her lively inner spirit couldn't quite be contained. Now they only reflected a dull, rather lifeless sheen. Had she been ill? Where was her natural sparkle? Hank's stomach turned over. This was not the woman who had left Thorp eight years ago.

They were staring at each other, and both of them realized it at the same moment. Jessie turned away and nervously hung the blouse back on the rack. "Is this accidental?" she asked in an undertone.

"Running into you? No. I stopped by the house. Mavis told me where you were."

Jessie closed her eyes briefly. Bob wouldn't like Hank coming around. More importantly, *she* didn't want Hank coming around. Just standing here beside him, she found that her heart was thudding and her palms felt clammy. It was a shocking reaction and too reminiscent of how Hank used to affect her. "Please don't do that again."

"I had to see you."

Stealing a quick breath, Jessie faced him again. She immediately began revising her initial observation of him looking exactly the same. His hair was still untamed, but much shorter than he used to wear it. And there were some silvery strands mixed in with the black. He'd aged some, not as much as she had, but some.

Suddenly aware of her thinness and that she wasn't pretty anymore, Jessie hugged the package of nightgowns to her small bosom. "No, you didn't have to see me. There's no reason for you and me to see each other. I really must be going."

She walked away. Hank felt glued to the floor for a moment, then followed. He stayed behind her until Jessie had gone through Cleavers' front door, then he fell into step beside her. "I only want to talk to you, Jessie."

"We have nothing to talk about."

Hank tried to laugh. It was a good attempt, but it came out rather hollow and humorless. "We could discuss the weather, couldn't we?" When she didn't answer, he stopped her with a hand on her arm.

She backed up, her eyes wide and startled. "Don't touch me!"

A flush heated Hank's face. "What's wrong? You're so different. Have you been sick?"

There were people on the sidewalk, and along with a few hellos, Jessie and Hank were drawing some very interested stares. "Please leave me alone," Jessie whispered. "Just leave me alone!"

Hank stood there and watched her hurrying down the street. He felt like he'd just been slapped. What had he expected from Jessie? Maybe a decent hello and a few words of normal conversation were too much to hope for, considering their past, although that seemed rather ridiculous after all this time. But he never could have imagined this kind of reaction. She'd acted almost afraid of him. Afraid of *him,* not of his old reputation and what people might think.

Rubbing his mouth reflectively, Hank kept watching until Jessie got into a car at the curb. His mind reached for reasons for her strange behavior. Nothing made a whole lot of sense. A jealous husband? A long illness?

It made his stomach churn to wonder if maybe Jessie just couldn't stand the sight of him.

Jessie battled tears during the short drive home. Seeing Hank had been a demoralizing blow. It wasn't his intense good looks that had struck her so hard—although they were indisputable. It was his vibrancy, his aura. Hank had always overwhelmed her with his strong, confident personality, and obviously, nothing had changed in that regard. To be fair, though, he hadn't displayed any of his old cockiness. In fact, he had seemed unusually serious, almost somber.

She didn't really understand Hank's mood or the degree of her own shock at seeing him, but Jessie knew the meeting had been emotionally shattering.

Sniffling a little, Jessie carried the package into the house. Mavis appeared at once. "You had a caller."

A determination to provide no more fodder for Thorp's gossip mill sprang from somewhere within Jessie. "Did I?"

"Hank Farrell."

Jessie formed a smile. "He probably just wanted to say hello." She held up the package. "I found some nice gowns for Ann. I'll bring them up to her." Jessie started up the stairs.

"You mean Hank didn't find you at Cleavers?" Mavis called out.

Pretending not to hear the blunt question, Jessie kept on going. She had actually forgotten how nosy people were in Thorp. Today's reminder pointed up the wisdom of keeping her unhappy marriage to herself, Jessie thought as she rapped once and entered Ann's bedroom.

Ann Shroeder was a small, pretty blonde with warm, blue eyes. She smiled expectantly. "I see you bought something."

Jessie laid the package on the bed. "Four granny gowns. Believe me, you'll be well covered in any one of these."

Ann opened the package and took the gowns out, one at a time. "They're great, just what I wanted. Thanks, Jessie."

"You're very welcome. I enjoyed shopping for them." Jessie wandered around the room, finally stopping at a window. Moving the lacy pink curtain aside, she looked out on Front Street. While she and Ann were far from confidantes, Jessie truly liked her sister-in-law and felt that the two of them were becoming close. Until this summer, Jessie hadn't known her brother's wife all that well. Ann was from Wyoming, but her hometown was about a hundred miles from Thorp. Since Jessie had been living in California during Ann and Bob's marriage, this was really the first opportunity for her and Ann to spend any amount of time together.

"Something wrong, Jessie?"

Jessie hadn't spoken her private thoughts to anyone for years, other than in the sessions with her counselor. She hadn't always been so reticent, but eight years of hell had inflicted a lot of damage on what had once been a friendly, open personality. But the questions she'd thought of the other day about Hank—if he was married, especially—were eating at her.

Leaving the window, Jessie sat in the chair beside Ann's bed. "After I left the house today, a man came by and asked for me. Ann, have you met or has Bob ever mentioned Hank Farrell to you?" Jessie saw a slight start of surprise on Ann's face. "You know who he is, don't you?"

Ann set the stack of nightgowns aside and began folding the wrapping paper into a neat square. She spoke with gentleness. "I know who he is, yes. I've seen him around town and heard things." Her blue eyes radiated kindness. "You and he . . . I'm not hinting for details . . . but there was something important between the two of you at one time, wasn't there?"

Jessie felt memory prickling her spine. She sensed that Ann did not share Bob's prejudicial opinion of Hank, which was understandable. Ann hadn't been around Thorp during Hank's feverish courtship and the Shroeder family's ill will toward him. Oddly, that she had someone in her own family now who might discuss Hank without ingrained negativity brought tears to Jessie's eyes. She quickly blinked them away, not wanting this to turn into an emotional scene.

"Hank wanted me to marry him," she said huskily. "Everyone, Mother, Dad, Bob and most of the town, was down on him. He was—" Jessie drew a troubled breath "—pretty wild. He ran with the wrong crowd, the people who didn't seem to give a damn about much of anything."

"And you turned him down."

"Yes, I turned him down."

Ann reached for Jessie's hand. "Apparently you loved Allen more than Hank, Jessie," she said softly. "I'm so sorry your marriage didn't work out."

Jessie felt like a band had just been tightened around her chest. She could see why Ann had said what she did, but it wasn't in Jessie's power to explain anything about her marriage. Although, seeing compassion and sympathy in Ann's clear blue eyes, she wished it were.

It just wasn't possible, though, and Jessie realigned her thoughts. "Ann, Mavis told Hank where I had gone, and he came to Cleavers."

"Oh, I see." Ann smiled. "Well, what did you think? Hank's a very handsome man. Is there still some of the old spark between you?"

Ann was kind and sweet, but she was so very, very much in the dark. First of all, there hadn't been just a "spark" between Jessie and Hank; there had been a blazing inferno. Secondly, there was no way Ann could know the devastation of Jessie's marriage, which totally eliminated her even suspecting the trauma Jessie was still fighting on a daily basis.

For a moment, Jessie was at a loss for a reply. There was so much going on inside her, feelings, emotions, memories, questions. Somewhere in the past eight years of pain and misery, she had lost her confidence. Sadly, she had also lost her innate sense of honesty. She had learned to lie, to pretend, to wear an impassive, unemotional mask, for anything else, any hint of the woman she kept burying deeper and deeper within her own psyche, trying to preserve an impossible peace, had resulted in another horrible scene with Allen.

It was habit now to show nothing of her thoughts, and she was able to state calmly, "I doubt very much if anything's left between Hank and me, but he surprised me today. I couldn't imagine why he wanted to see me, and...well, I left him standing on the sidewalk."

"Then you didn't talk to him at all?"

"I couldn't. I was stunned to even see him."

"I see. And now you have questions."

"Yes, I do."

"I'll tell you what I know, Jessie. He never married. He has women friends, but I've never heard of anything serious. I have heard that he's quite successful with his many ventures. He lives on the old Farrell ranch, but from what people say, Hank has improved it a great deal. He raises excellent German shepherd dogs and Appaloosa horses. Rodeo bulls, too. He also owns a helicopter and operates a charter service."

Ann's information was so foreign to the Hank Farrell Jessie was familiar with, she could hardly believe they were talking about the same man. The fact that he had never married created a dull ache in her heart. *If I can't have you, I'll never marry anyone, Jessie.* That's what Hank had said eight years ago, at their final meeting when she had told him she was going to marry Allen Vaughn.

Listening to Ann, Jessie felt sick to her stomach. She had made such a mess of her life. Why had she been so positive about Allen and so confused about Hank? Her parents, her brother and so many other people in town had shunned Hank, and she'd let their pressure influence her. Bob hadn't said it right out for a long time, but Jessie knew her brother still didn't like Hank.

Feeling nauseated, Jessie got up. "Is there anything you need, Ann?" The sympathetic look on her sister-in-law's face made Jessie feel like weeping. She knew now that she had a real friend in Ann, and that was comforting. But there was so much Ann didn't know, and Jessie wasn't ready to talk about it. Not yet. She really needed to be by herself, to think about and attempt to digest Ann's information.

"Nothing, Jess," Ann replied softly.

"I think I'll take a walk, then."

"You go right ahead."

"I'll see you later."

"Of course."

Jessie left the bedroom with tears in her eyes. It was self-pity she was feeling, she knew, an emotion she rarely indulged in. Even through the worst of the bad times with Allen, she had avoided self-pity. But there was something so immutably sad about learning that the man she had really loved and been afraid to marry had, more than likely, been the better choice.

Slipping out of the house without running into Mavis, Jessie left the Shroeder yard and started down the sidewalk. She walked fast, as though she had a destination or an important appointment.

Thorp had a small park. Avoiding the play area with its swings and slides, Jessie made her way to a far bench and sat down. When she was growing up, the park hadn't existed. The town was gradually progressing, changing, just as she had changed, just as Hank had. Why hadn't she been able to see beyond Hank's youthful recklessness? Why had she listened to her family? Why had she been swayed by Allen's smooth line? Oh, yes, she'd been very impressed with the Vaughns' money and life-style.

She'd been a very shallow young woman, hadn't she?

Jessie gave a sharp, bitter laugh. Her eyes had certainly been opened to the world and she was no longer young. In years, yes. Thirty wasn't old, by any means. But she felt much older. She had no sense of innocence anymore, Jessie realized sadly. Or hope. To her, the glass was no longer half full, it was half empty.

She had no dreams, either, no just-out-of-reach visions that kept a person young and excited. Some people were still young at seventy because of dreams.

What had her dreams been about, those girlish fantasies of so long ago? Jessie smiled then, a nostalgic, ironic tug of her lips. Her dreams had been about Hank Farrell, that brash, swaggering, foolhardy young man who had made her laugh with a joke and tremble with a kiss.

Jessie's eyes glazed over as memory replaced the present. She had kept her and Hank's relationship at arm's length for a long time. At first, it had been easy to do. The summer she came home after her second year of college, though, Hank was no longer content with an uncomplicated goodnight kiss.

"We're not kids now, Jessie."

His arms were around her. The moon was bright and reflected in Hank's eyes. Instead of taking her home after a drive to Casper and a movie, he had parked the car in a secluded spot just outside of Thorp.

"You know I love you," he whispered against her lips.

"But you want too much."

"I want you."

By the end of that summer, her resistance had evolved into a guilty secret. Those uncomplicated kisses hadn't been enough for her any longer, either, and while she was still battling her family about Hank, she was seeing him every chance she could find. And they were making love.

"Let's get married, Jessie. Please don't leave and go back to school."

"I have to. Hank, don't do this to me."

"Are you ever going to marry me?"

"I... don't know."

He got very angry, very quickly. "You'll make love with me, but you won't marry me. Why?"

She began crying. "You know why. Hank, you do such crazy things. Why did you get into that fight with Kurt last week? The whole town's talking about the two of you fighting all over the street like a pair of hoodlums. And why do you drink so much and drive through town like you're on a racetrack?"

"Do I do those things when I'm with you? Jessie, they don't mean anything. If this town wasn't stuck in the dark ages...! Damn, I hate gossiping busybodies!"

"They wouldn't have anything to gossip about if you'd behave! Hank, you don't give anyone a chance to know you the way I do. How can I defend you to my family when all they see is that other side of you?"

"I don't want you to defend me to anyone! I'm who I am, and I love you. You love me, too. Why do you care what anyone else thinks?"

Sighing, Jessie lingered on that question. Why *had* she cared so much what other people thought?

The answer was so simple, and yet so complex. Like Hank, she'd been who she'd been. At seventeen, nineteen, even at twenty-one, she hadn't been able to ignore either her family's or the town's opinion of Hank.

That November, in college, she met Allen. For two years she dated Allen in Cheyenne during the winter and Hank during the summer. It wasn't a deliberate deception. She kept trying to break it off with Hank, but every time she even got near the subject, he would take her in his arms. Her weakness for Hank was like a sickness, an addiction. Her relationship with Allen was completely different. So very different . . .

Children's laughter and shouts penetrated Jessie's thoughts, and she shook off the past and smiled wistfully at the group playing on the swings. She had so many aches and regrets where Allen was concerned that her unfulfilled desire for a child was really only one more.

But, sometimes, like now, it surfaced and stung with tremendous force. Allen had refused to even discuss the subject of children. And Jessie had learned very early in her marriage that insisting upon anything with her husband could cause one of his terrifying rages.

She hadn't known him at all before the wedding. During three long winters in Cheyenne, she had been doing nothing but shadowboxing with a man who had managed to keep his true nature a complete secret. His family had known about his instability, which was why Allen was attending school so far from California. Jessie had learned, after she was married and trapped and desperately afraid of her husband, that his family had allowed her to marry him without knowing his faults.

It was a transgression Jessie couldn't forgive, even though the Vaughns had tried very hard to make it up to her. It was because of Allen's parents' help and emotional support that the divorce had finally become a reality. And they had insisted she accept a generous monetary settlement, too.

Jessie hadn't had the strength to argue about it. The money was in a bank in California. At the present, she couldn't see herself ever touching it, but she also knew she had to do something with her life. She owned half of the Shroeder property in Thorp and had also inherited some cash at her parents' deaths, which Allen had forced her to hand over to him. He hadn't needed it, but it had been a way to keep her dependent on him. At least, that's what the counselor had told Jessie. It made sense, certainly as much as anything else did about the past eight years.

That moment when she'd heard Hank's voice in Cleavers returned, and Jessie closed her eyes to completely recapture it. Hank had been shocked by her appearance, hadn't he? By her thinness?

She'd never been voluptuous, but her figure used to be nicely rounded. Hank had always said she was beautiful, but she wasn't beautiful now.

Jessie wiped away a tear. She should have talked to Hank. That's all he'd wanted, just to talk. When he'd touched her arm, she had nearly jumped out of her skin, a ridiculous reaction.

Did he even know her marriage was over?

Frowning, Jessie realized that probably no one in Thorp, other than Bob and Ann, knew. Neither one of them were gossips, especially about family affairs, so Mavis probably didn't even know.

Rising, Jessie slowly started walking toward home. Should she try to see Hank? He might not want to see her again after her rudeness today. Besides, she looked so different.

What would another meeting accomplish, anyway? Only more memories gnawing at her, and did she need that now? Attempting friendship with Hank seemed so anticlimactic. They'd never been just friends. Even at the beginning, there'd always been that special thread of sensuality between them. It had astonished her, frightened her, and then, for a period, overcome her. Pretending it hadn't existed was impossible.

No, she wouldn't try to see Hank. It was best to leave the past alone, just as she'd demanded on the street today that Hank leave her alone. Before the end of the summer, she would figure out what she wanted to do, and if she happened to run into Hank again, she would merely say a normal hello and go on about her business.

After a steak and salad that evening, Hank sat in the hot tub and thought about Jessie. Why was she so thin? So nervous? Why would she refuse to even say a few friendly words to him? She certainly didn't think he would try anything personal with her, did she? She was married, for crying out loud. Didn't she know him better than that?

Hank shook his head disgustedly at such a moronic progression of thoughts. In the first place, the Hank Farrell Jessie had to remember wouldn't have hesitated so much as a heartbeat to forget about her marriage. Was that what she'd been afraid of? Had she thought he was planning a fast move?

That wasn't why he'd gone looking for her, and he would have told her so if she'd given him the chance. He'd just wanted to see her, and deep down, he, himself, didn't really know why it had been so imperative. He knew only one thing for sure: he'd have to be pretty damned stupid to ask for a repeat of the kick in the teeth Jessie had given him eight years ago.

But damn, Jessie bothered him. She'd changed so much. It was really a wonder he'd recognized her.

No, that wasn't true. He would recognize Jessie anywhere, anytime. So what if she'd changed? He had, too. Some crazy kind of wildfire used to burn in his body. He hadn't been able to drive fast enough or drink enough beer or give anyone enough sass to extinguish it. He'd been hot and excitable and ready for anything.

Nowadays, his favorite pastime was sitting in a hot tub. Hank grinned wryly. If that wasn't change, what was?

Maybe Jessie would like him better now. Not that she hadn't liked him before. Hell, she'd loved him, hadn't she?

Hank frowned. He didn't know anymore *what* Jessie had felt back then. Maybe he'd been so swept away by her, he'd only *hoped* she had felt the same. After all, she sure hadn't married him. She'd married that creep, Allen Vaughn.

There was something about that guy that had made Hank's skin crawl when he'd met him. Hank would never forget that day. Jessie had graduated college in May and come home in June. Only, she hadn't come alone.

"Hank, I'd like you to meet Allen Vaughn. Allen, this is Hank Farrell."

He saw right in Jessie's eyes that it was over between them, but he wouldn't believe it.

Jessie sensed his fury. Her voice was nervous, but determined. "Allen, I need to talk to Hank for a few minutes. You don't mind, do you?"

She took Hank's arm and led him out to his car. "I'm going to marry Allen. I wrote you a letter—"

"You didn't say anything about getting married!" He clasped Jessie's hands in his. "Jessie, you can't mean this."

She pulled her hands away. "I've tried to tell you for years, Hank, but you would never listen."

"Tell me what? That I drive too fast? Christ! You're going to marry that jerk because I drive too fast? Jessie, can't you see how dumb that sounds?"

"You'll meet someone else, Hank. You'll get married, too."

"Never! If I can't have you, I'll never marry anyone!"

Nothing he'd said had changed Jessie's mind. She'd gone away and married Vaughn. Hank supposed she'd been happy these eight years, but something had given her that strained, scared-rabbit look. What was it?

Hank realized suddenly that he had very little basis for even generalized speculation on Jessie's life. Other than her living in southern California, he'd heard nothing about her in eight years. The Shroeders didn't talk about their own, and as far as Hank knew, Jessie hadn't kept in contact with any of her girlfriends.

Which was mighty strange, now that he thought about it. Why hadn't he ever questioned that before? A few of Jessie's old friends still lived in Thorp, and they certainly weren't above spreading a little news around town. There should have been *some* information being passed around about Jessie in all that time.

For eight years, it was as though Jessie had dropped off the map. Bob was so damned tight-lipped, anything he knew about his sister would die when he did. But other people around town should have heard something from her!

Hank lunged up out of the tub. There was something terribly wrong here and he wasn't going to pretend there wasn't! Jessie didn't look well, and if she was suffering over something, he wanted to know what it was.

Leave her alone, hell! He wasn't going to leave Jessie alone at all, not until he found out what had been going on the past eight years. She wasn't even a tiny bit happy! That's why her eyes didn't sparkle and why she'd lost so much weight.

Drying off as he went, Hank headed for the house. He was going to get to the bottom of this, come hell or high water!

Three

―――

"Tonight?"

"Right now. I'm coming over to pick you up."

Jessie glanced uneasily over her shoulder, half expecting someone to be watching and listening. No one was. Bob was upstairs with his bedridden wife, and Mavis was audibly banging pots and pans around in the kitchen. Jessie had answered the phone on its first ring, having coincidentally been in its vicinity at the moment.

"Why, Hank? What for?" she whispered.

"For God's sake, don't be afraid to be overheard talking to me. I'm not sneaking around anymore to appease your brother or anyone else. I want to talk to you as a friend, and I sure don't see any crime in that."

Jessie listened to her own apprehensive heartbeat for a moment. Only a few short hours ago, she had decided friendship was impossible for her and Hank. But here he was, offering it. Confusion wracked her.

Hank, apparently, wasn't the least bit confused. "I'll be there in ten minutes. You can watch for me, or I can ring the doorbell, whichever you prefer."

The connection was broken and Jessie slowly put the phone down. Why, after the way she'd treated him today, was Hank so insistent on seeing her again? And why the haste?

According to Ann, he wasn't married or seriously involved with anyone. Maybe he *did* know about the divorce. Maybe...

Her imagination was getting carried away! There was nothing left of the old excitement between them, nothing! And even if Hank did have some kind of weird hope of picking up where they'd left off, she certainly wasn't receptive to any such shenanigans!

Still, Jessie's hands went to her hair in a completely female gesture. She hadn't looked in a mirror since long before dinner, and she had to need some repairs.

Recalling that Hank had said ten minutes, Jessie dashed upstairs. She quickly dragged a brush through her hair and applied lipstick to her pale mouth. She still looked drawn, strained, so she brushed a little blusher on her cheeks. After a spritz of perfume, she grabbed a sweater, then hurried back downstairs.

She couldn't just leave, she realized. The house would be in an uproar if she just disappeared after dark. Jessie walked into the kitchen. "I'm going out, Mavis."

The heavyset woman turned away from the sink. "Out?"

"For a walk."

"Alone?"

Jessie lifted her chin. Mavis's eternal curiosity was becoming annoying. "Please tell Bob if he should ask. I won't be long." Ignoring the dubious expression on the housekeeper's face, Jessie left the kitchen, walked through the house to the front door and let herself out.

She was shaking, she realized, as if it were cold outside, when, in fact, the evening was only pleasantly cool. It was because she didn't understand what was going on with

Hank, she decided. There were other factors, too. Her own bad nerves were enough to keep her on edge, even if she didn't have so many ambivalent memories of Hank to deal with. Then there was Bob, who wouldn't be at all thrilled with her slipping out of the house to meet Hank Farrell.

Not that Bob was mean or anything. She truly loved her older brother. He was tall and handsome and a dear, if a trifle stodgy. But he was so extremely protective of her. He had always been that way, from as far back as Jessie could remember.

And he had never liked Hank. The only real arguments between her and Bob had been long ago and about Hank. Sad as it was, Bob had thought—and maybe still did think—the world of Allen. Jessie knew her brother didn't understand her divorce. She'd mumbled something about incompatibility and he hadn't questioned her, thank goodness. Jessie could only lay that oversight on Bob's own deeply-ingrained concern for his wife and unborn child. He wasn't ordinarily so easily fooled.

Jessie opened the iron gate, closed it behind her and began walking toward the corner. She snuggled her sweater around her shoulders, shivering even with its warmth.

She had no idea of what to say to Hank or what he might say to her. He'd sounded so stern on the phone, so determined, and she didn't know why. If his mood had something to do with their earlier meeting, she couldn't figure out the connection. Unless he was angry at her abruptness and wanted to tell her so. Would he do that?

If he did, if he really only wanted to yell at her, what would she do, take it or yell back?

God, she really didn't have a whole lot of fight left in her anymore. If Hank wanted to fight, heaven forbid, she'd probably humiliate herself by collapsing into a sobbing heap.

The residential street was completely quiet. Jessie had once known who lived in every house. Bob had pointed out the places with new people, some of whom had merely moved from other areas of Thorp.

Front Street was the prettiest street in town, with the nicest houses and the oldest, most stately trees. Jessie had loved living there as a girl. She had liked her father being the town's banker and her mother being involved in every civic endeavor.

Maybe she had been a snob, she unhappily mused now. She had been discovering a lot of negative things about herself since the onset of the divorce and entering that counseling program. Kelsy Worth, her one-on-one counselor, was an intelligent, straightforward young woman who pulled few punches. Kelsy wouldn't dream of condoning a physically abusive spouse, but she had also made Jessie look at herself honestly. It was becoming something of a habit, Jessie was beginning to realize.

The hardest part of the whole thing was trying to find her positive traits. "You've got them," Kelsy had insisted. "After eight years with an overbearing, abusive husband, you're just not accustomed to displaying them. Or even recognizing them. Keep working on it. You'll find yourself again, Jessie."

Would she? In the middle of a sigh, Jessie's pulse leapt as the headlights of a vehicle appeared on her street. It was a pickup truck, she saw after a minute, and when it slowed down in front of her house, she knew it was Hank.

Jessie waved and the truck came on and stopped at the curb beside her. The passenger door was pushed open. "Hi," Hank said softly.

She got in and pulled the door closed.

"Aren't you going to say hello?"

She stared straight ahead, unable to respond in kind to his teasing tone. "I don't understand this."

"You came."

"Did you give me a choice? I hardly want a ruckus on the front porch."

"Meaning there'd be a ruckus if I dared to come by when Bob is home?" When she didn't answer, Hank shook his head, put the pickup in gear and started it moving. "I'm not going to lose any sleep over Bob not liking me, Jessie. Our relationship has nothing to do with him, anyway. It never did.''

"He's my brother."

"Does that give him the right to run your life?"

Jessie was shaking harder than ever and attempting to hide it. "I don't want anyone running my life, including you."

Hank knew what she meant. He'd been pretty forceful on the phone. "Maybe I sounded demanding, but only because you would have refused to see me if I'd called all sweet and sugary."

Jessie gave him a quick, bemused glance. "You've never been sweet and sugary in your entire life."

"Oh, yes, I was. With you, I was. Maybe you've forgotten how it was with you and me, but I haven't."

Jessie pulled her sweater tighter. "What did you want to see me about?" She heard Hank chuckle softly.

"Don't want to talk about the past, huh?"

"No, I don't. If that's why I'm in this truck, just turn it around and take me back home."

Hank cut the small talk and fell silent, but he didn't turn the truck around. Instead, he headed straight for his place. He wanted Jessie to see it, anyway, and they could talk a lot better in the house than in this old truck. He should have taken the car, Hank thought, and grinned inwardly. His late-model Mercedes sedan just might surprise Jessie.

Jessie caught on to their destination just before they reached the Farrell driveway. "Hank, I'm not going to your house with you! Why would you even think such a thing?"

"What's wrong with going to my house? Would you rather go to Merrill's?"

"Of course not!" Merrill's was the most popular café in town. "But just drive around ... or something."

"Still sneaking around where I'm concerned, Jessie?" He turned into his driveway, stopped the truck beside the house and turned off the engine.

Jessie couldn't answer. "Sneaking around" was exactly what she had done with Hank, and sitting in the quiet night with him now told her why she had defied her family to do so. After all this time and all that had occurred, she was still aware of Hank's appeal. The same stirring, disturbing feelings he had caused years ago were roiling within her now, not as strongly and distinctly as before, but definitely there. And she wasn't sure exactly what that meant. Beyond danger, that is. Not physical danger, not like she'd endured with Allen. But these feelings should constitute a warning all the same, Jessie knew with a troubling uneasiness.

If Hank thought otherwise, if he really had orchestrated this meeting to attempt some sort of familiarity, he was in for a rude awakening.

"It's been eight years, Jessie, and I want to know what happened to you during those years."

"I beg your pardon?" Her voice was a weak croak. That was the last subject she could have imagined Hank bringing up. Evidently, her ego hadn't been completely destroyed by Allen, not when she'd just been associating Hank and familiarity!

Well, this was worse than any kind of personal move, and what in God's name had brought this ghastly subject to his mind?

Hank turned in the seat to face her. Being close enough to Jessie to touch her was like a small miracle. It had been so long, and old memories were bombarding him: Jessie in his arms, Jessie's lips swollen and sensual from their kisses. There were more, and not all of the memories were good. Some of them hurt like hell and cautioned him. But it still seemed utterly fantastic to be sitting beside her again.

"Jessie, after you ran off today, I got to thinking about a few things that don't add up. How come you never stayed in contact with any of your friends? How come no one in town ever knew anything about you? I would have heard, you know. If anyone had known anything about you, it would have gotten around town."

"You have no right to question me." Jessie shut her eyes in a wave of utter agony. Allen had thrown a tantrum the first time she'd attempted to write to anyone in Thorp other than her family. She had dared to argue, which had resulted in a stinging slap on the face, not her first, either. Already, after only a few weeks of marriage, she had been slapped twice. At the time, she hadn't understood what was happening. In her world, people didn't slap other people, especially someone they supposedly loved.

"Is there something wrong with those questions? Why would you object to answering them? Jessie, it's like you disappeared. Didn't you ever think people might wonder?"

"I...wrote to my family regularly," she said in a strange, hoarse voice. Which was true, although Allen censored every letter. Actually, it wouldn't have changed anything if he hadn't. She never would have written a word about being mistreated by her husband. She was so ashamed and worried that she was doing something wrong, that she wasn't handling her marriage well, she couldn't have told anyone.

"But what about your friends? Why did you cut yourself off from them the way you did?"

She couldn't stand to be interrogated this way, especially by Hank. If anyone could trip her up and get her to say things she didn't want to, it was Hank. His old ability frightened her; he knew her too well.

Jessie's only refuge was anger, which she didn't have to pretend. There was enough anger residing within her that it wasn't at all difficult to let some of it show. "Why do you suppose?" she asked hotly. "You must have some big idea in that head of yours. Just what are you thinking?"

Hank was silent for a long, brooding moment. "I wish to God I knew," he finally growled. "You're different, Jessie. I can't lay a finger on it, but there's something damned wrong. You're not happy. Are you and your husband having problems?"

Jessie couldn't answer right away. Her conjecture that he knew about the divorce had been way off the mark, but how did he have the gall to ask such a question? What made him think he could barge into her private life this way?

And then she remembered that Hank had never lacked audacity or been reluctant to barge into anything. Hank might have changed a lot, but some traits were apparently immutable. Like his magnetism, for example. She had hardly looked at him, but was so conscious of his presence in the truck, it was as if some kind of force field was battering her senses.

She didn't want to tell him about the divorce. She didn't want to even touch on the subject, not when she had so much to keep from him and anyone else in Thorp who might hope for details. Only Hank wasn't like anyone else in Thorp. He never had been, and Jessie couldn't pretend not to recognize his differences. No more than she'd been able to ignore them when he had started showing interest in her years ago.

He was staring at her, silently demanding a reply. "I'm divorced," she said after enduring his incessant, probing gaze for as long as she could.

Hank froze. "You're what?"

"I'm divorced."

He was staggered, suddenly choked with shock. The past eight years rose up and nearly strangled him, the frustration, the anger, the sorrow. His voice was harsh. "For how long?"

In an effort to appear calm, Jessie was looking beyond the windshield, vaguely registering the dark shapes of buildings and the fence that paralleled the driveway. She'd anticipated questions, which she had no intention of answering, but this one was innocuous enough. "It's been final for about a month now."

There was a long stretch of tension-filled silence. Hank found himself battling an onslaught of bitterness. It was all for nothing, all the pain, the heartache, the sleepless nights. Her marriage was dead, and why in hell had they all had to go through it? Jessie hadn't deserved a bad marriage, and he sure hadn't deserved what he'd gotten. Hank even felt pity for Allen Vaughn, when he'd never once thought of the man as anything but a jerk in the past eight years.

He finally spoke, and there wasn't a whole lot of life in his voice. "Why didn't you tell me that this afternoon?"

A small, weary sigh escaped Jessie. "For what reason?"

Hank exploded. "Jessie, for God's sake! I still—"

"No!" Jessie covered her ears, blocking out whatever he was trying to say. But she knew what it was, even if she didn't hear it: he still cared for her. How could he? Tears burned her eyes.

"Jessie..." Hank slid closer and saw her squeeze against the door.

"Don't touch me!"

"My God, what happened to you?" Hank quickly lost any generous feelings he'd had for Allen Vaughn. Whatever was haunting Jessie was Vaughn's fault! "What did that bastard do to you?"

Her voice was thick with tears. She couldn't deal with this. She wasn't *ready* to deal with this. "Take me home."

Hank's mind began spinning in a new tack. She was divorced. She was *free!* It didn't seem possible, and yet she'd told him so herself. This wasn't rumor, it was fact. He hadn't yet completely assimilated the information; that would take some time. But she was no longer Vaughn's wife!

Dazed but certain he didn't want to take her home yet, Hank pleaded. "Jessie, come in the house and have a cup of coffee. Let's talk, please."

She was sitting so rigidly her spine ached. And so close to the door, one of the handles was digging into her side. "I'm not going to talk about my marriage with you, so if that's what you're thinking..."

"I don't care what we talk about. Just don't shut me out."

She became defensive and sent him a challenging look. "What do you want from me?"

Hank felt like crying. It had all been for nothing, and his mind was going in circles, with all of the events of the past eight years swirling like so much dust in a whirlwind. "Do I have to want something?" he asked unsteadily, then added, "Maybe I do want something, but even I don't know what it is. I only know that you're here and it feels right. Don't ask me why. I'm as confused as you are right now."

She felt fresh tears gathering. She couldn't abide the sadness in Hank's voice. He wasn't accusing, but she felt herself drowning in guilt. She'd ruined his life. She'd ruined her own life. She couldn't take this another second.

Pushing the door open, Jessie stumbled out of the truck, looked around wildly and made a dash for the highway. It took a second for Hank to spring to life. She'd surprised him. He never could have anticipated Jessie running off into the dark.

He caught up with her at the end of the driveway, and when he grabbed her, she came at him screaming and kicking. He was panting by the time he had subdued her with purely superior strength. "Jessie, Jessie, stop it," he chided as he clamped her up against himself and she still continued to try to get away. She was crying and cursing, saying words he'd never heard come out of her mouth before.

He held her so tightly, she finally gave up. But there was no defeat in her posture; there was only resignation that he was the stronger. He felt like bawling while he stood there. She was so tiny and thin, nothing at all like the soft, full-bodied girl she'd been.

But she was still Jessie, and everything male in him responded to holding her. He couldn't help it. He felt heat and life in his loins, even though he knew very well that she was in no mood for anything even remotely connected to making love.

For a moment, he basked in the feeling. No other woman had ever given him the sense of wonder Jessie did. With Jessie, something opened and flowered within him and at the same time, something soft and intimate closed around them. Hank wasn't a poet, but Jessie had always lifted his thoughts to a higher plane than he really understood.

Her unhappiness was palpable, creating disquietude in him, drawing him away from Jessie's femaleness and bringing him back to the grim present. "I'll walk you back to the truck and take you home," he said gently. She made no answer and he released her slowly and took her hand. "You're safe with me, Jessie. Don't you know that?"

She only released a shuddering sob, but she let him lead her back to the truck. Hank helped her up onto the seat and closed the door. Then he walked around the front of the truck and got behind the wheel. He cast her a worried glance while he started the engine and saw only the back of her head; she was staring out the side window.

He drove to town slowly, searching for the right thing to say. She couldn't take any more questions, he knew, although his brain was deluged with them. That SOB Vaughn had done this to her, but Hank couldn't figure out how. Had the man been a womanizer? A cheat? A liar? What could a man do to a woman to hurt her so terribly? This was something more than a case of the blues over a divorce, but what?

They reached Front Street much too quickly for Hank. He parked at the curb and left the engine running, wishing to God that he could take Jessie in his arms and comfort her. All he dared use was words, though, and he spoke very softly. "I'm sorry, Jessie. I didn't mean to upset you."

She believed him. Hank had been a lot of things, but he'd never, ever been unkind to her. "It wasn't your fault. Good night, Hank." She reached for the door handle.

"Will you see me again?"

She hesitated. "I . . . don't know." She took a sniffling breath. "I hurt you before. I don't want to hurt you again."

Tears filled his eyes. All of the heartaching moments he'd lived through during the past eight years were suddenly trivial compared to the here and now. Jessie's unhappiness was as close to tangible as emotion could be, and he'd borne his own a lot easier than he could bear hers. "Then see me. The only thing that would hurt me is a refusal to see me."

Jessie hesitated again. Her face was swollen from crying, and she had to look like the wrath of God. And yet Hank was looking at her as if she were the most beautiful woman on earth. How could he? He didn't understand, and she couldn't explain, and it was all so terribly sad.

But she felt his strength, all the same, and while it might be selfish to draw upon it, she desperately needed something strong in her life. "All right. Call me," she whispered.

"I will. Do you want me to walk you to the door?"

"No."

"Good night, Jessie."

"Good night." Jessie got out of the truck and opened the iron gate. She heard the idling engine of the pickup until she went through the front door and knew Hank was waiting until she was inside.

Her heart felt like it weighed a ton in her chest. She knew she wasn't through weeping. She'd never really thought that Hank might still care for her or that he had truly suffered over their breakup. Oh, she'd known that he'd been angry and frustrated when she married Allen, but Hank had always seemed to be so well fortified, so able to deal with reality. And he'd known, just as she had, that their affair had to eventually end.

That final winter, her letters had been different. Hank's replies had evidenced his refusal to accept her cooling affections. Which wasn't completely accurate, either. It wasn't that she had lost her feelings for Hank, but permanency with him had simply been out of the question.

What a fool she'd been.

The sounds of the television set in the master bedroom reached the upstairs hallway. Jessie walked on past the door, intending to go right to bed.

"Jessie?"

She stopped and turned. Bob was in the hall, closing the door to his room behind him. Jessie saw his eyes narrow on her tear-smeared face. "What's wrong? Where did you go?"

Right at that moment, he looked exactly like their father, Jessie noted in the back of her troubled mind. She was really so very weary of doing what other people expected of her, of living by others' standards. What was wrong with her own standards? She'd never had secret cravings to do bad deeds, to lie or cheat or steal. Why was there always someone around watching her every move?

She was thirty years old, and if one wanted to get down to hard facts, this house was half hers. Bob had no right to question anything she did. Did she ask him where he'd been when he got home late?

In spite of some clear thinking on the matter, Jessie avoided her brother's eyes. She wasn't going to lie, but her spurt of courage only went so far. "I was with Hank Farrell."

"Hank Farrell!" Bob muttered a curse. "Why in hell were you with him?"

Jessie's hands came up in a fluttering plea. "I can't talk now. You'll be home tomorrow. We'll talk then." Leaving Bob standing there with an awful scowl on his face, Jessie turned and fled to the privacy of her bedroom. She locked the door, which she never did, switched on a light and then weakly sank onto the room's one upholstered chair.

She was trembling from head to foot, and she hugged herself and rocked back and forth. She knew she had to pull herself together. Kelsy had impressed upon her how crucial self-help was. "Professional help is important, Jessie, but in the end, it will be up to you."

In a disoriented, nebulous way, Jessie likened her situation to treading water in a vast, endless sea. There were a few ships out there, but none she really wanted to reach. Treading water all alone was dangerous, but so was revealing herself.

Kelsy had advised telling her family everything. "Your brother should know, Jessie. From what you've told me, I feel that Bob loves you very much. Protectiveness in older brothers is perfectly normal."

The thought of confession was abhorrent, though. Every time Jessie tried to work up the courage to tell Bob the truth, she nearly died inside.

Now she visualized the same thing with Hank and cringed at the picture in her mind. No, she could never tell Hank about it, never. She would get over this alone, by herself.

Later, in bed, Jessie thought about Hank still caring for her. She didn't imagine his feelings as love, not after all this time, but how could he even have any affection for her after what she'd done to him?

Turning her face to the pillow, Jessie wept for Hank. She would see him again, she had to. In spite of Bob's disapproval, Hank was the only ship out there with any meaning. His instinctive, "You're safe with me, Jessie. Don't you know that?" was like some kind of lifeline. She simply did not have the strength to deny it.

Mavis had Sundays off, so Jessie cooked breakfast the next morning. To her amazement, she had awakened hungry. It had been so long since food had had any appeal, Jessie was delighted with the hunger pangs in her stomach. She prepared bacon and eggs and toast and coffee, and began arranging a pretty tray for Ann.

Bob came into the kitchen. "Good morning."

"Good morning, Bob." Jessie sent her brother an anxious smile. "How's Ann this morning?"

"Hungry. She can't have bacon and eggs, though."

"Just this once? For a special treat?"

Bob shook his head. "Sorry, but no, Jessie. It's oatmeal and fresh fruit for her. We're following Dr. Haley's orders to the letter this time."

"Of course," Jessie murmured, regretting the impulse to cook for everyone in the house just because she was hungry. Sliding the platter of bacon and eggs into the oven to keep warm, she got a small pan out of the cabinet for the oatmeal.

"I can do that. You go ahead and eat."

Jessie smiled hopefully. "Can you eat with me this morning?"

Bob hesitated, then nodded. "Sure. I'll take Ann's tray up, then join you."

Together, they made the oatmeal and prepared Ann's breakfast tray. Bob took it upstairs, and Jessie set the table for two. She knew conversation about Hank was inevitable, but she was going to do her best to stall it until after she and Bob ate.

Bob was tactful enough to enjoy the fine breakfast without controversy, Jessie noted gratefully while she ate until she was stuffed. Then they pushed their plates back and refilled their coffee cups.

"May we talk now?" Bob asked quietly.

"Of course," Jessie agreed. She felt much calmer this morning. Last night, she couldn't have talked about Hank with Bob if her life had depended on it.

"Why do you like Hank Farrell, Jessie?"

"Why do you *dis*like him?"

Bob's dark eyes bored into her across the table. "It goes way back. Hank's a maverick, a loner, a square peg in a round hole. He's never fit in."

"With what, Bob?"

"With what! With Thorp, with people, with anything!"

"He has friends. They're not your friends, granted, but I'm sure he has friends. At least, he used to. You tell me. Does Hank have friends now?"

"Jessie, that's immaterial. The kind of people Hank attracts are not your kind. *Hank's* not your kind. That's all I'm trying to get across."

"I see." Jessie took a sip of coffee and returned her cup to its saucer. She lifted her eyes to her brother's. "I'm thirty years old, Bob. Do you really think I still need a keeper?"

Bob's face flushed. "You don't want my advice."

"Your advice, yes. Your censure, no."

"You're going to see Hank again."

"Yes. I'm sorry you disapprove, but yes."

Bob stood up and dropped his napkin onto the table. "I don't understand you. How could you leave a man like Allen and then take up with the likes of Hank Farrell?"

"Oh, Bob," Jessie whispered, shaken to her very soul. For the first time, she felt a genuine urge to blurt out everything. But Bob had dropped his bombshell and left the kitchen. Jessie could hear him going upstairs. She sat there for a few stunned minutes, then got up to clear the table.

Nothing was ever simple, was it?

Bob and Ann were so happy with each other, neither of them could possibly understand a truly disastrous marriage. Bob didn't even handle divorce cases in his law office, so he had no experience with the trauma of broken relationships.

While Jessie washed the dishes, she realized her brother's opinion of Allen was understandably limited to their personal association, which had been very little. She would have to accept that or tell Bob the real facts of her marriage.

As for his dislike of Hank, it seemed nothing short of immature to Jessie for Bob to still be harboring ill will after all these years. Why on earth hadn't the two men become at least speaking acquaintances? Surely Bob wasn't petty enough to be deliberately clinging to memories of Hank's old infractions, was he? Obviously, from what Ann told her, Hank *wasn't* still the maverick Bob had just proclaimed him.

Sighing, Jessie admitted Bob's similarities to their father again. Robert Shroeder had been a good and decent man, but he had believed in and insisted upon a strict code of behavior. It had certainly influenced Jessie, and she was beginning to see how strongly it had influenced her brother, too.

Well, this was one time she was going to follow her own instincts, and she needed Hank's kindness now, desperately needed it.

In trying to dissect what Hank seemed to exude, Jessie decided it was reassurance. Hank had always had such an incredibly stubborn inner strength, marching to his own drumbeat in spite of most of the town's common rhythm.

The fact that he still retained some of his old feelings for her seemed secondary to the reassurance she needed now, Jessie realized. She was far from ready to think about anything beyond that with any man, even Hank.

But if he was willing to settle for friendship, she was going to absorb it and thank him for it.

She only wished Bob wasn't so opposed to *any* kind of relationship between her and Hank.

Four

Mick didn't work at the Farrell ranch on Sundays, which gave Hank several hours of routine chores to take care of by himself. This morning, he was glad of the solitude. He had a lot on his mind, and while Mick might have listened, Hank wasn't sure he could discuss Jessie with anyone.

He fed and watered the dogs, then put the adult animals in segregated runs for some exercise while he washed down their kennels. There were a half dozen litters in varying stages of growth, and he stopped to inspect the handsome pups. Mick was a marvel with dogs and had played a big role in Hank's decision to raise and breed them. The venture had turned out to be extremely profitable.

With the most pressing daily tasks out of the way, Hank took a tour of the pastures. His Appaloosas, with their unique coloring, were splendid horseflesh and difficult to come by. Appaloosas didn't breed true. That is, an Appaloosa mare bred to an Appaloosa stallion didn't necessarily produce an Appaloosa foal. Thus, the Farrell ranch contained a mixture of breeds, some Arabians, some Spanish, some ordinary cow ponies. With careful record keeping and a watchful eye, Hank had been producing some extraordinary Appaloosas in the past few years.

The rodeo bulls were another point of pride. Ugly, humpbacked animals, it took careful crossbreeding to produce bulls that were ornery enough to satisfy the buyers. Hank was really only just getting off the ground with that enterprise, but he had some young stock that was beginning to draw attention.

The entire ranch was profitable, no question about it. It took specialization these days, Hank firmly believed, although he raised a nice herd of ordinary beeves, too. With all of the diversification, there was always money coming in from some direction.

Looking over his property, which included a helipad and hangar for his helicopter, Hank heaved a strangely discontented sigh. He was making money and he liked his methods of earning it. But he wasn't content. All of his friends were married, most of them with children. *His* house was empty.

And, dammit, so was he.

Jessie filled his mind. They could have had so much together. If only she had married him instead of that Vaughn character.

Shaking his head, Hank started for the house. It was all water under the bridge now, and it was senseless to constantly rehash it. Which was what he had done most of the night. It only hurt to dwell on the sweet, gentle Jessie he'd loved to distraction eight years ago, and it was fruitless to curse events that were over and done with. What he had to concentrate on now was just how involved he wanted to get with Jessie again.

Maybe the real question was, could he stop himself from getting involved, even if he decided it was best not to? He'd felt the depth of Jessie's need last night, even if he couldn't distinctly define it, and he certainly didn't understand its cause.

The crux of Hank's dilemma was gnawing, unignorable fear that he might fall as hard for Jessie as he had before. Unquestionably, they were both different people than they'd been. But there were enough remnants of old emotions to worry him. At least, there was in him. Look at how holding her last night had affected him. As for Jessie, he couldn't tell. She was so lost in whatever was haunting her, he'd picked up only unhappiness from her.

But she had agreed to see him again, and he had sensed some kind of reaching out at their parting. That's what kept getting in the way of common sense.

He owed Jessie nothing, certainly not another piece of his soul. But neither could he turn his back on her, not when she seemed to need a friend worse than anyone he'd ever seen. He would just have to be careful and get in only so deep.

At eleven, Hank went to the house and dialed the Shroeder home. Before the call could go through, though, he had second thoughts and put the phone down. Raking his heavy, dark hair with agitated fingers, he questioned his own sanity. Why not leave well enough alone?

He felt so on-again, off-again about this. If it was anyone other than Jessie, he would walk away. There was trouble on the horizon, and he could feel it approaching and threatening his peace. But it *was* Jessie, and he couldn't get her unhappiness out of his mind. Was it possible to make her smile again? To laugh at some corny joke? What had gone on in her marriage to put her in such a condition? Would she talk about it today?

After a long, brooding stare at the telephone, Hank finally grabbed it and redialed. It rang twice, then Jessie, herself, answered, saying, "Shroeder residence."

Hank's shoulders tensed. Even her voice affected him. "Hello, Jessie."

"Hank. Hello."

"Are you all right this morning?"

"I'm . . . fine."

He only half believed her, but he responded with, "Good. It's a beautiful day. How about a drive somewhere?"

Jessie felt the house's silence. Bob was with [obscured] with Mavis absent, there were no sounds of [obscured] cooking. A drive would be a pleasant way to sp[obscured] the afternoon, and with Bob home, Ann wouldn't need Jessie for anything.

But it wouldn't be just an ordinary drive. She would be with Hank. Jessie's pulse beat a little faster as she thought about it. Hank represented solidity right at the moment, but there was more, she knew deep down. The fact that he still cared for her wasn't possible to completely overlook, although she was in no frame of mind to expand on it.

"Jessie?"

She wasn't sure. Last night, she'd been sure, but today, his voice was doing some strange things to her. And she really didn't want to be a bother to Hank. "You're sure it wouldn't interfere with anything?"

"Interfere with what?"

"You must have your own ways of spending Sunday afternoons. What do you usually do?"

Hank cleared his throat. He spent some Sundays with one woman or another, but he wasn't about to be that honest. A small alarm went off in his head when he realized that with Jessie around, the other women he knew had suddenly lost appeal. It wasn't a comfortable feeling and he evaded the whole subject by turning the tables on Jessie. "I'll tell you what I've been doing every Sunday for eight years, if you'll tell me what you did."

Jessie instantly clutched the phone tighter. She might have overreacted last night to Hank's questions, but there was no guarantee she wouldn't do it again, should he press her. If that's what was in his mind, it would be better to forget spending the afternoon together. "You *are* kidding, aren't you?" she said rather stiffly, giving him the opportunity to laugh it off or to tell her point-blank what he was planning.

"Sure, I'm kidding," Hank replied with some dryness. "How about the drive? Do you have other plans?"

Jessie had grown away from unilateral decision making, and she uneasily realized that even something as seemingly nocuous as taking a drive with an old friend had hordes of disturbing subtleties. Would she ever really trust her own judgment about anything again?

Until she knew, she would have to rely on honesty as much as possible, Jessie decided. "No other plans, Hank. I just don't want to disrupt your life." That was very true and easily related, if not in a completely steady or positive voice.

She sounded troubled again, Hank noted, although, even without seeing her, he could tell she was a long way from the emotional state she'd been in last night. He relaxed a little. "You're not disrupting anything. If I didn't want to take a drive, I wouldn't have suggested it."

Jessie hesitated again, but only briefly. Hank's confidence was reassuring, exactly what she needed. "All right, I'd love to see some of Wyoming again."

"We could get closer to the Tetons, if you'd like."

"Any direction would be fine, Hank."

"How about if I pick you up in an hour?"

"I'll be ready."

"See you then." Hank put the phone down, then frowned at it. Was it possible for him and Jessie to be only friends?

He gave his head a disgruntled shake and got to his feet. This was dangerous business. Even after eight years, he wasn't free of the old Jessie. He knew it now with every cell in his body. He could feel it, taste it, and it was a scary sensation.

With his hands dug into the back pockets of his jeans, Hank went to the window and stared out. He'd loved her so much, and he'd gone through hell after she married Vaughn. Slowly, too damned slowly, the agony had made him lose his sharp edges. He'd buried himself in work, *lots* of work.

Hank snorted out a hard, cynical laugh. At least one good thing had come out of it: he'd made a success out of his ranch.

Dressed in jeans, a red blouse and flat shoes, Jessie rapped at the door to the master suite and entered when she heard, "Come on in, Jessie."

Bob and Ann were both propped up with pillows against the headboard, with the Scrabble board on the bed between them. Ann smiled cheerily. "Would you like to play?"

"No, thank you, Ann." Jessie approved of her brother's casual attire, a baggy, comfortable-looking gray sweatsuit. Unlike their father, who had seemed to enjoy exchanging his bankers' suit for less-restricting garments, Bob rarely relaxed his dress code. "I'm going out for a few hours, and I wanted you both to know."

Bob's expression cooled. "With Farrell?"

Jessie met her brother's eyes. "Yes. He's picking me up in a few minutes."

Ann's smile contained warmth. "Have a good time, Jessie."

"Thank you." Jessie's gaze stayed on her brother, but he was studying his game tiles very intently.

Much too intently. Sighing softly, Jessie looked at Ann. "We're just going for a drive. I'll see you this evening, if not before." She saw a lovely understanding in Ann's eyes, something she would give a lot to see in Bob's.

Jessie couldn't believe Hank's car. "I thought we'd be in your pickup. That's why I wore these jeans."

Hank sent her a lazy grin. "Something wrong with jeans?"

Jessie glanced at his, then wished she hadn't. If jeans hadn't been invented for men with Hank's build, they should have been. His belt encircled a taut, firm waist, and his long thighs were beautifully, sensually muscled. Along with the dark blue jeans, he wore a white shirt and black cowboy boots. With his coloring, his head of thick, almost black hair, his tanned skin and vivid blue eyes, he was utterly, almost unbelievably handsome.

Quite abruptly, Jessie faced front. "I like jeans as well as anyone else," she mumbled, much too shaken over Hank's good looks to ignore the sensation.

Out of the corner of her eye, she saw him take a pair of sunglasses from the visor and settle them on his face. Glad that she, too, had thought to bring dark glasses along, Jessie went into her purse for them.

Then she sat back and told herself to stop being so darned silly. Wasn't it only natural to appreciate striking masculinity? When she stopped doing that, she might as well throw in the towel.

Oh, damn, she was confused, Jessie admitted miserably. She wasn't looking for anything other than friendship from Hank, and if he should even attempt to go beyond that, she'd probably fall apart. But why, *why,* should noticing how really handsome he was upset her so much?

As she'd told Hank, she really didn't care what direction they took for the drive, so when he headed south, she made no comment.

After a few miles of silence, Hank glanced her way. "Ten dollars for your thoughts."

Having vowed to do her best to enjoy the day in spite of inner unrest, Jessie shaped a smile. "Has the price of thoughts gone up that much around here in eight years?"

"Inflation is out of control."

"Apparently."

Hank kept darting her glances. Her thinness disturbed him, although there was a certain elegance to her body, too. In fact, if he was meeting Jessie for the first time, he'd probably think she was gorgeous and not question her weight. Even that troubled quality in her dark eyes was mysteriously attractive. If he didn't compare her to the Jessie he remembered so well, she was one beautiful lady.

It was just that he missed her old sparkle.

"I've got a lot of questions, Jessie," he said quietly.

Jessie tried to appear unaffected, but this was what she had feared. "I'm sure you do, but please don't ask them."

Hank let a few moments go by while he digested the request. Although she was definitely calmer today, she was still stubbornly opposed to unrestricted conversation. Why?

That attitude didn't make sense to him. "Will you answer just one?"

"I'm not sure. What is it?"

"It's a relatively simple question, Jessie. Why do you object to talking about your marriage?"

"Simple?" Jessie laughed uneasily. "You do get right to the point, don't you?"

"Did I get to the point? I'm in the dark, Jessie. I don't even know when I'm getting close to something that's important to you. I don't know you anymore."

That was truer than he could even imagine. Jessie looked out the side window and watched the countryside they were speeding past. Pastures alternated with vacant, sagey desert, productive ranchland with large expanses of unused, sometimes unusable wasteland. Wyoming contained diverse scenery, some breathtakingly beautiful, some bland and boring. She loved it all, Jessie realized behind more urgent thoughts concerning Hank's remarks. She loved this immense, open country far more than she could ever care about California.

Funny, she'd never realized that before.

"Obviously, you're not going to comment on that."

Jessie turned her head to look at Hank. "Eight years changes a person. That's why you feel you don't know me anymore."

"It's a lot more than that," Hank scoffed. "Don't lie to me, Jessie. I can accept silence on some subjects, but not lies."

Embarrassment pinkened Jessie's cheeks. She didn't have the gall to deny that her observation had been a ploy to conceal the truth. Instead, she went deep into the past. "You never liked lies, did you? I remember that about you very well."

That was true. For all of his misbehavior, he'd never been able to abide lies or liars. But Jessie going into the past at all was much more intriguing than a discussion of ethics. Hank cocked an eyebrow at her. "What else do you remember about me?"

He was teasing and he wasn't. There was something challenging in his voice, something daring her to remember. And she did remember, Lord help her. She remembered too much! Jessie took a startled breath. She never should have given him this opening.

He didn't let her reluctance to speak go by. "How about the time we were on this very road in my blue Dodge? Do you remember that?"

"Jessie, if you do that for very long, we'll end up in the ditch!"

"Is that why you took this road, to remind me of that?" she whispered. Then, louder and with some tension, "No trips down memory lane, please."

Hank shook his head grimly. "No questions, no memories—what are we supposed to talk about, Jessie?"

Jessie's mouth dropped open at the sharply cynical note in his voice. "You're angry!" She took a moment to formulate her thoughts. "Maybe I don't blame you. Maybe you have every right to anger. But if you feel that way, why did you look for me yesterday? Why did you insist on seeing me last night? Why are we in this car together today?"

Hank drew a deep, almost shuddering breath. He'd gone too far, but Jessie was an enigma and he was having trouble with that image of her. "I'm sorry. I'm trying to figure things out, and I guess I'm not doing a very good job of it. Let's forget it, okay? It's a great day for a drive, and there are lots of things to talk about. In fact, we don't have to talk at all, if you don't want to." With a flip of a button, Hank turned on the radio, which was tuned to a country station. The familiar voice of Willie Nelson filled the car. "Still like country?"

Jessie nodded stiffly, not quite past Hank's anger. As she'd said, she didn't blame him. Hadn't she cried for him last night? One didn't get over the kind of hurt she'd inflicted on him very easily, and apparently he'd lived with anger these many years, which was perfectly understandable.

She felt terrible, which she hadn't expected during this drive. Last night, she'd absorbed Hank's kindness, his reassurance, his strength, like a thirsty sponge, and now she knew that those qualities weren't the only ones that Hank possessed. Like her, if for entirely different reasons, he was full of pain.

"I brought it all back, didn't I?" Jessie said huskily, on the verge of tears. "I'll bet you rarely thought of me anymore, and then I came back. I'm sorry, Hank. I needed to get out of L.A. so badly, I didn't think about what my return to Thorp might do to you."

Hank slowed the car for a sharp curve. "Did you ever think of me at all, Jessie?"

"Yes, I thought of you. A lot of times."

"Did you know I stayed single?"

"No. I didn't know any more about you than . . ."

"Than I knew about you."

With a heavy sigh, Jessie leaned her head back. Oddly, her tears had fled. In their place was a dull resignation. She was still hurting Hank, she didn't understand her own feelings, and she wasn't very happy about their interaction. "I wouldn't have contacted you, Hank," she said quietly. "I wondered about you, but I never would have made the first move."

Hank turned down the volume on the radio. For the first time, he sensed some genuine honesty from Jessie. But the blame for that meeting in Cleavers was his, not hers. "I accept the responsibility of my own actions. I wanted to see you."

Jessie adjusted the position of her head against the rest so she could look at Hank. "Do you wish you hadn't?"

His eyes found her, then returned to the road again. After a minute, he veered to the shoulder and pulled to a stop. Putting the shifting lever in Park, he turned in the seat and leaned forward. "What do you want me to say, Jessie?"

"The truth," she replied softly. "I'll understand if you regret contacting me." His eyes were hidden behind his dark glasses, but she felt their impact in a sudden rush of adrenaline. He was so glowingly handsome, and she hadn't once hoped or assumed that he wasn't tied to someone. How had that happened? *Why* had that happened? After she left, there must have been dozens of women who would have jumped at the opportunity to get close to him.

His expression altered very subtly, just a faint movement around his mouth. But Jessie's heart swelled with nostalgia. Every nuance of voice and gesture was familiar to her. She hadn't remembered every tiny detail about Hank, but today was bringing them all back. Through the privacy of her dark glasses, she watched his mouth while he spoke.

"I can't give you the truth, because I don't *know* the truth. I'll be as honest as I can be, Jessie. I'm going both ways on this. One minute, I'm so damned glad you're back in Wyoming, I can't see straight, and the next, I'm sick-to-my-stomach afraid."

"You have a right," she said hollowly, on his side in this. Who had a better right to ambivalence?

"Maybe, but it's a little more complex than that, too. Your refusal to talk about the past eight years is damned puzzling." Hank sat back, took off his glasses and rubbed his eyes. "You know, Jessie, you're not the first person who's gone through a divorce. Half the people I grew up with have had the same experience, and not a one of them isn't willing—hell, *eager*—to talk about it."

"Heaven help them," Jessie whispered.

Hank faced her again. The glasses were still in his hand, and his blue eyes were dark with emotion. "I want to be your friend, Jessie. I want to help you. But how can I when you're so secretive?"

Jessie tore her gaze from his. She didn't want to lie to him, but he needed to hear something. "What do you want to know?"

Hank's pulse gave a funny little leap. "You'll talk about it now?"

She could skirt the truth, the really bad times. She could speak in generalities. "We . . . didn't get along."

"Did he cheat?"

Did he? Jessie didn't care if he had or not. She'd had no evidence of other women, but she hadn't been looking for any, either. Maintaining peace had been her only goal, her career, her first thought every morning, her last every night. "That wasn't the cause of the divorce."

Hank studied her. "You just didn't get along." She was lying or at the very least, evading something.

"It happens," she said huskily.

Anger flared in Hank again, but he kept it contained. He would learn nothing from Jessie about her marriage until she was ready to talk about it. If ever. "Yes, it happens," he mumbled.

It hurt that she was so closed to him, so guarded. For a moment, he thought of turning back, of returning to Thorp and dropping her off. But then he visualized the rest of the day. There was always work to do on the ranch and he'd found a lot of comfort in physical labor.

He wouldn't work today, though, he knew. He would wander the house or the grounds and think about Jessie.

Without comment, he put his glasses back on, slipped the car into gear and resumed driving. He heard a deep, heart-rending sigh from Jessie and knew that she'd grasped his mood, his knowledge of how she'd dodged the truth.

This isn't helping her, he realized in a burst of empathy. Whatever disorder and doubts churned within him, pressuring her would only amplify the problems she was struggling with.

And then it came to Hank. They were strangers! That beautiful, tempestuous, forbidden love affair in his memory had happened to two other people, to another man named Hank and another woman named Jessie. Any connections with that series of stormy events were weak and flimsy, barely discernible.

He drew in a long, shaky breath. If he was to help Jessie, they had to start over. He had to leave the past alone. Did it really matter what had caused that haunted look in her eyes? It was over, whatever it had been.

He cleared his throat. "Have you ever ridden in a helicopter?"

Jessie's head jerked up. Bogged down with remorse and sadness, she hadn't expected a change of subject. Gratefully—and wisely—she took Hank's cue. "Ann told me you have one. When did you take up flying?"

"It was six years ago this summer. With the big oil slump, a lot of equipment hit the market at rock-bottom prices. I saw an article in a newspaper about a flying service going out of business and holding an auction. Casper was hit pretty hard, you know. A lot of businesses went under. Anyway, I went and took a look at their inventory and ended up buying one of their helicopters."

"*Before* you knew how to fly it?"

Hank grinned and nodded. "Impulsive, huh? I signed up for flying lessons and commuted to Casper for about six months. It was great. I took to flying right away. There's nothing like it, Jessie. It makes you feel so free, as if you could go on and on forever."

"Free," she murmured. "Sounds wonderful."

"I'll take you up anytime you want to go." There was time yet today, but maybe just driving along and talking was best for today. He told her about his helicopter, its make, its age, its capabilities. "I get a lot of business from real estate agents," he continued. "There's hundreds of miles of ground to cover in this area and apparently, potential buyers appreciate a look at property they're considering from the air."

"That makes sense. Ann said you raise dogs."

"German shepherds. Beautiful animals." He sent her another smile. "You'll have to see the pups. They're the cutest things you've ever seen."

"Who do you sell them to?"

"Pet stores, mostly, although other breeders are a good market, too. Someone's always coming around looking for a strong, healthy animal. You have to keep introducing new blood to the line." Hank chuckled. "The record keeping is phenomenal. Every animal is registered with several different agencies, so its lineage is unquestionable. It's quite a business."

"And you keep all of those records yourself?"

"I have a computer."

"*You* own and operate a computer?" Jessie looked at him in amazement. "I'm impressed, Hank."

He hadn't opened up to impress her, but her admiration was gratifying. If he would have impressed her this way years ago...

No, he wasn't going to start thinking like that again. They were talking normally, and it felt good. "Let me tell you about my Appaloosas."

An hour later, they were still talking. As they approached the outskirts of a small town, Hank asked, "Are you hungry?"

Jessie hadn't been thinking about food. She was so wrapped up in the man Hank had developed into and his many ventures, she hadn't thought about herself in any way, shape or form for miles and miles. It was a tremendous departure from what she'd grown accustomed to, and startling, when she realized it.

And she *was* hungry, which, again, delighted her.

Five

Hank stopped at a café with at least two dozen cars parked around it. "Looks like a lot of people eat Sunday dinner out around here," he commented on their way into the busy restaurant. A woman behind the cash register pointed out a vacant table, and Hank led Jessie to it.

"I think I feel like a hamburger," Jessie remarked absently while scanning the menu.

"You don't *look* like a hamburger."

Her eyes lifted. She had completely forgotten that silly joke. Hank used to follow that oft-repeated and totally inane observation with, "But you do look good enough to eat." Today he only smiled at her.

She responded with a soft smile of her own. "This is nice, Hank," she said, closing the menu.

He thought about his discontent that morning and realized it was gone. He was wonderfully content right now, sitting in this unpretentious little café with Jessie. "Yes, it is." His gaze flicked over her red blouse. "I always liked you in red. But then, I guess I liked you in anything, didn't I?"

The waitress saved Jessie from a stammering reply. They ordered hamburgers, french fries and coffee. When the man at the next table said hello and struck up a conversation with Hank, Jessie stayed uninvolved and used the opportunity to study Hank.

His personal remark had caught her off guard. How should she interpret it? As a compliment? A reminder of their interwoven pasts? If it had been intended as a reminder, he had used too mild a verb. *Liking* could hardly describe what they had felt for each other. The whole subject made Jessie uneasy and she retreated from it and concentrated on the man across the table as he was now.

No one could doubt that Hank belonged in Wyoming. His rangy build, the squint lines at the corners of his eyes, the ease with which he wore Western clothing, his speech, everything about him was pure Wyoming. The friendly man knew it, and so would anyone else who understood the area.

Wyomians were a special breed, tough, inured to harsh weather and hard work, fiercely proud of their heritage and state. What on God's green earth had drawn her to Allen and California? This was where she belonged, as much as Hank did. As much as the elderly rancher having Sunday dinner at the local café did.

Jessie's heart began to flutter with a shimmering excitement. She hadn't expected this feeling, this sense of really coming home, when she'd offered to spend the summer with Ann and Bob. But, oh, it was welcome. For the first time in years, she truly felt hopeful.

She had a college degree, and with some brush-up education, she could teach. Or, if that didn't work out, there surely were other jobs in and around Thorp. She could even open a small business of some kind if she couldn't find satisfactory employment.

The gentleman at the next table stood and reached for his check. "Nice talking to you, Hank."

Hank got to his feet and offered his hand. "Stop by the place if you get to Thorp, Don."

"Thanks, I will." After he'd tipped his hat to Jessie, the man walked away.

"Nice guy," Hank remarked as he resumed his seat. The waitress had delivered their coffee, and he took a swallow. His gaze locked with Jessie's and he saw something different in her eyes, a glow that hadn't been there before. He didn't know what had caused it, but he liked it. Very much.

He spoke softly, for her ears alone. "You're a beautiful woman, Jessie."

She colored. This was very definitely a compliment, and she wasn't comfortable with it, not when she knew how much her appearance had changed. "That's very kind of you, but I know how I look."

He smiled teasingly. "Are you going to sit there and tell me I don't know what's beautiful in a woman?"

She couldn't look at him. "I'm too thin."

"You could use a few pounds, but you're still beautiful. And don't argue with me about it."

His teasing tone tempered his words, and Jessie found herself giving him an embarrassed smile. "You always were very flattering."

"I was in love, Jessie, and anything I said to you wasn't for the sake of flattery."

He'd said that so quickly and in such a deadly serious vein, Jessie's heart nearly stopped. His mood had flip-flopped so fast, she couldn't assimilate the change. But she was stunned and instantly ill at ease.

"Don't look so disheartened, honey," Hank said quietly. "I'm not making a pass."

"No, you're reminding me of what I did to you," she whispered.

"Is that how you see it? I didn't mean it that way." He watched her lift her cup to her lips, noticing the slight trembling of her hand. "Jessie, I can pretend only so much. You know how I felt about you."

"We were kids," she said hoarsely.

Astonishment struck him. "Kids? I was twenty-five when you married Vaughn. I hardly think a twenty-five-year-old man can be categorized as a kid."

She had said the first thing that had popped into her mind, and it was so ridiculously weak, Jessie wished she could retract it. Of course, they hadn't been kids. Their relationship had started out when they had been in the kid stage, but they certainly had been old enough to know what they were doing at its demise.

Or they should have been. Heaven help her, she wasn't certain of anything anymore.

"Here comes our food," Hank said. "Let's talk about something else while we eat."

They were a good two hours away from Thorp, and it surprised Jessie that Hank didn't head back when they returned to the car. "Where are we going?" she asked as he turned south again.

"Nowhere in particular. Why? Are you anxious to get home?"

Jessie sighed and put her head back. She had used the restroom and had refreshed her makeup. There wasn't a reason in the world to hurry back to Thorp, but since that personal exchange in the café, she had wondered what Hank's next offensive would be.

He couldn't prevent his bitterness from showing sometimes, apparently. And maybe, if their friendship was going to endure at all, he had to get it out of his system. In spite of that, Jessie knew she didn't want to call a halt with Hank. He satisfied something lost and searching within her. Her loose ends weren't quite so noticeable in his presence, and staying on her toes with him—or attempting to—was resulting in one very positive reaction: she wasn't dwelling on the past eight years.

Besides, something quite wonderful had happened today. She knew very keenly now that California wasn't in her future. That was a tremendous decision and a giant stride toward getting herself back together. She had Hank to thank for that, even if he was completely unaware of his part in it.

Jessie watched him through the curtain of her eyelashes. Perhaps she should tell him about it.

She raised her head. Yes, he deserved to know that his effort today had resulted in something good. "Hank?"

He glanced at her. "I thought you were napping."

"I was thinking. I..." Talking about herself wasn't a simple matter. She began again. "I've been thinking about staying in Wyoming."

Hank's stomach tightened. "For good?"

He wasn't thrilled. Jessie's mouth went dry. "Maybe that's a bad idea."

Hank hadn't thought beyond the summer. Why he hadn't was perplexing now, but with Jessie's revelation, he knew that he'd been thinking only in terms of the present. Maybe he hadn't wanted to ponder the future, he mused. Maybe visualizing Jessie leaving again was too painful to contemplate.

No, that wasn't it at all. He'd honestly been so enmeshed in what was going on right now, he hadn't worried about events that were at least two months away.

It was something to face, though, and obviously Jessie had been giving it a *lot* of thought. It was almost impossible to place her in Thorp as a permanent resident. What would she do? Where would she live? What did that mean in terms of the two of them?

Hank's palms were suddenly clammy. "I didn't say it was a bad idea. You just took me by surprise."

An urge to cry was choking Jessie. Her plans looked cruel when associated with Hank. She'd only thought of herself again. What remnant of ego had made her think he would see her information as good news?

Dear God, why was everything so complicated? Biting her lip, she jerked her face to the side window, virtually turning her back on Hank.

He cursed under his breath. The road was paralleling a river, and periodically they had passed pulloffs with signs indicating fishing access. He watched for the next one, knowing it wasn't very far away.

When he saw it up ahead, he slowed down for the right-hand turn. Jessie realized he was going to stop. But she was still fighting tears and didn't want Hank to see them, so she kept her face directed away from him.

The car rolled to a stop and the engine was turned off. Jessie had no idea what Hank was going to say to her, but she was stunned to feel him slide across the seat and put his arms around her. Instantly, she froze. "Don't, Hank!"

He reached around her head and took her chin. "Look at me."

"I . . . can't."

"Yes, you can. Look at me, Jessie." He applied pressure to her chin and brought her face around. His eyes were dark and stormy. "I want to show you something." Before she could do more than gasp, his mouth covered hers.

She began trembling. His kiss wasn't harsh, but it was possessive. His mouth worked hers, played with hers, shaped hers. She couldn't breath, and with her eyes wide open and staring, she registered the man kissing her so intently.

Was she being assaulted? By Hank? The idea was preposterous, but his eyes were closed and she couldn't see his feelings. Was it a kiss of anger? Of bitterness? She didn't know.

He wasn't going to stop, she realized. Little or no response from her made no difference to him. He was kissing her to prove something, to *show* her something.

And maybe it was working. That is, if he wanted to show her that she wasn't immune to him, it was.

Her own heartbeat was betraying her, her own femaleness! And he wasn't above dirty tricks. The way his tongue slid along her lips was one that she remembered very well!

She moaned deep in her throat, frightened out of her mind. How could he incite such a response from her when she had learned to abhor physicality of any sort?

He wasn't Allen; she was rational enough to realize the difference. But he was a man, and she didn't want to want any man!

Only, she did. Almost-forgotten sensations of desire were exploding within her. It had been too long since she'd desired even a hint of contact with a man, and Hank—his scent, his size, his lips and arms—was pushing her way, way over the line of self-protective restraint she'd been living behind.

Her eyes squeezed shut at the same moment her lips parted. Hank groaned and threaded his hands into her hair. This was Jessie, sweet, beautiful Jessie, and he couldn't stop kissing her. His tongue slipped into her mouth, touching hers, teasing hers. He felt her hands come up and slide around him and then, as though uncertain of where to land, travel the length of his arms to his wrists.

The movement lifted and pushed her breasts into his chest. His blood surged hotly, and he sought a more satisfying position by enfolding her in a tight embrace and bringing her body closer to his.

"Jessie, Jessie," he hoarsely whispered against her lips. He stole a hasty, much-needed breath of air and pressed his mouth to hers again.

But Jessie's head was free to move this time and she tore her mouth away. "Why are you doing this?" Her voice was so gravelly, Hank hardly recognized it. Sanity struck him hard and fast. He hadn't kissed Jessie for pleasure, but that's what it had evolved into, the most intense pleasure of his life.

He moved away from her and fell back against the seat, breathing hard, his chest rising and falling laboriously. "I'm sorry. I had some crazy idea of showing you...something." Hank groaned. "I guess I'm the one who got shown."

Jessie was weak, leaning against the door, breathing with difficulty, too. She knew her face had to be flushed, for she was hot all over. Her skin burned, and she wished she could shed her blouse and jeans to cool off. Especially her jeans. They felt too tight and suffocating. She squirmed, and then squirmed again when she saw that Hank's jeans were too tight, also.

Much too tight.

She quickly averted her eyes. "I think it's safe to say that we both got shown," she mumbled thickly. "Although, frankly, your reasoning escapes me."

It was escaping Hank, too. But he was calming down enough to try and recapture what it was he'd been thinking before he'd made that blatant and completely unnecessary pass. What had he been doing all day, waiting for some kind of sneaky opportunity to kiss her? To see if it would feel the same as it used to?

It didn't. It had been hotter and wilder than anything they'd ever done before, and their lovemaking had been hot enough in the old days.

Damn! Talk about behaving like a jerk!

"I thought..." He paused, aggravation obvious in the way he raked his hair. "I don't know, Jessie. Maybe I needed to prove something to myself. Last night, when I held you, a lot of old memories came back."

"And you wondered if there was anything left between us."

"Yes...no." Hank shook his head. "No, I didn't wonder about that. I wondered about a lot of things, but not that."

"You wondered about me and what I wouldn't talk about," she said wearily.

"Yes. Most of the night, in fact." Swiveling in the seat, Hank put his hands on her shoulders. At her wincing reaction, he said softly, "Don't worry. This isn't another attempt to show you something, honey. I don't even remember what was in my mind."

"You were upset because I told you I was considering staying in Wyoming," she reminded none too gently.

They stared into each other's eyes. Hank finally broke the strained silence. "Why would I be upset about that?"

"Oh, Hank, let's not play games. Not about that. You have every right to be upset at the idea of me living in Thorp again. It's your town now, not mine."

"Is that what I'm doing, playing games? I don't think so, Jessie. And I'm not upset about you moving to Thorp permanently. It just surprised me." He felt a wave of tenderness for her and removed his hand from her shoulder to gently brush a wisp of hair from her cheek. "You move anywhere you want to, honey. Thorp's no more my town than it is yours."

He was so real and big and alive. So warm and handsome, and he'd once meant so much to her. Jessie looked into his electric-blue eyes and acknowledged their ongoing jolt to her system. She hadn't liked being touched, but Hank was touching her and she loved it. She'd thought she would never respond to a man again, but she was still responding to the wild and wonderful kiss he'd given her.

How had she changed so quickly? Was she less afraid than she'd been? A little more confident? This man, whom she hadn't believed in, this man, whom she'd turned her back on eight years ago, was at the heart of her emotional progress. Guilt stormed her, along with some old fears. Dare she trust her own feelings with a man again, even with Hank?

He'd done well financially and apparently had settled down. But behind those incredible eyes, beneath that bronzed and sexy skin, he had to retain some of his old devil-may-care traits. And dare she risk her own mental health and the few positive gains she'd made since the divorce in a personal relationship with any man?

It was very easy to fall back into the sorrowful pattern she'd been enduring, and the kiss and Hank's intense chemistry scared the hell out of her. Last night and even most of today, she had ignored her awareness of Hank's drawing power. But he'd had to prove it, to *show* her how thin the veneer of self-control really was!

Well, he'd shown her, all right. And she wasn't capable of handling such explosive feelings.

She didn't even want to try.

"I think we should start back," she said with some coolness.

Hank's eyes narrowed. He was relatively calm again, although he knew it would take only one small sign of assent from Jessie to resume the pace of what that kiss had started. "You're mad at me. Don't you believe that your decision to stay in Wyoming only surprised me? Or are you mad about being kissed?"

Jessie slumped. She didn't want to get into a long, involved discussion about this. Hank would only be hurt if she tried to explain why she didn't want his kisses. Hurt and very curious, and it was really his curiosity she didn't want to arouse again. "I'm not mad. I just think it's time we started back."

He didn't want to let her get away with such flagrant evasion. She was a master at evasion, something she'd picked up during her marriage, obviously. Hank privately debated the point for a moment, and questions about Allen Vaughn seared his soul. What, why, how?

He conceded to her wishes, merely because to rebut them would cause additional friction between them. "All right, we'll head for home." He slid back across the seat and started the car.

Driving north, with Jessie silent and seemingly brooding, Hank's thoughts remained back at the river. Jessie had been startled by the kiss, but she had melted into it, nonetheless. He hadn't expected such an overwhelming onslaught of fireworks. Kissing Jessie had always been exciting, but there was a new dimension to the pleasure now.

He'd started something today that wasn't going to evaporate just because it would be best if it did. Where were they heading, he and Jessie? His desire to help her was sincere, but so was the voice in his head that kept advising caution.

Was that what he'd needed to show her, that they were both treading on pretty dangerous ground? That there were too many traces of what they'd once had still hanging around, and that those old feelings were bound to surface now and again in spite of any and all efforts to rebuff them?

If he could have exactly what he wanted right now, what would it be? If Jessie weren't so mixed up, if she had returned to Thorp divorced and not unhappy about it, would he ask her out and hope that something serious would result? Bottom line: if she were the same woman she'd been, would he have the guts to risk his heart and soul in another relationship with her? Would he *fall in love* with her again?

The conjecture made Hank squirm. Wanting her sexually didn't constitute love, and he would never give his heart so freely again, he knew. In her eight-year absence, he'd had no problem with keeping his feelings for women under control. With Jessie, the thought of control was almost laughable. He vacillated so much, it was sickening. He said one thing and thought another; he'd kissed her to prove something that had totally escaped him in the heat of an ominous passion.

And when she'd looked happy for a few minutes, apparently over her decision to stay in Thorp, what had he done? Encouraged her? Supported her? That *was* a laugh. He'd made her feel guilty, as though she had no right to invade his turf! What kind of jerk had he turned into?

It wasn't going to happen again. He wasn't some wet-behind-the-ears kid who couldn't keep a lid on his emotions. And he wasn't going to turn his back on Jessie, either. She still needed a friend, and she *had* a friend. Hank Farrell!

"Let's clear the air, Jessie," he said quietly.

"Can we?" she asked listlessly.

"Absolutely. No more passes, no more questions, no more digging into the past. Do you know what a friend is? He's a person who likes you unconditionally, just the way you are. He doesn't probe and pry and judge. He doesn't undermine your decisions with veiled negativity or outright disapproval.

"Last night, I offered you friendship, and today everything I've done would scare anyone off. Maybe today had to happen. Maybe we had to go through some dissension to reach a better understanding. Maybe I'd have to be a saint to paint everything rosy between us, and a saint I ain't, honey. Which you probably know better than anyone else.''

Jessie's thoughts had been troubling and convoluted, touching on her arduous marriage, but mostly going farther back. To a younger Hank. His kiss today had rekindled old, long-unused fires. She had become extremely jumpy about a man's touch, even something so innocuous as an accidental jostling in a crowd.

But she hadn't forgotten what true passion was like, that melting of bones sensation, that liquefying of organs and muscle, that tingling of skin, that *need*.

Now he was denying it, clarifying his position of friend, and she should be grateful. Instead, unsettling, ambiguous ghosts with hot breaths and searching hands persisted in badgering her. She watched the man behind the wheel through clouded, introspective eyes while he spoke. His words rang true: he believed in what he was saying.

She could only go along with it. To disagree would take a healthier foundation than she possessed. She was just beginning to regather strength of will, and to dispute Hank's reasoning would require more pluck than she had.

Today had been real, the most normal interaction she'd been a part of in years. If she didn't have so much to hide, they would have gotten along famously, even with so many echoes of their past relationship influencing their moods.

She saw him shoot her a questioning, uncertain half grin. "You know, it just occurred to me that I never asked if you *wanted* a friend. I felt you needed one, but I should probably ask. Maybe you'd prefer being left alone."

Jessie felt blood rushing to her head in a dizzying surge, while her heartbeat went crazy. Not want a friend? Not want Hank in her life? She never would have sought him out, but he was now an important part of her very existence! The thought of dissolving their fledgling friendship was nauseating, frightening.

She dampened her suddenly dry lips with the tip of her tongue. "No, I don't prefer being left alone," she said huskily. "I appreciate your...interest. Your friendship."

The flick of her tongue had cut through Hank like a hot knife through butter, resulting in a startling jolt to his nervous system. Maybe including Jessie in his assessment of treading on dangerous ground was erroneous; maybe it was only him.

Why did she still affect him this way? Why was she becoming more beautiful, more desirable by the minute? She was secretive, guarded and taut. Putting it in harsh, nakedly realistic terms, he knew women who were prettier and loved to laugh. Women whose problems were left at home when they dated.

Decisions about maintaining control were absurd. He wanted Jessie more than he'd ever wanted a woman, more than he'd wanted her eight years ago. His body ached with the knowledge and with what he had provoked with that kiss.

His throat felt dry and scratchy. The insistent, demanding rhythm of his own pulse beat was a torment. They hadn't cleared the air at all; he could only attempt to pretend otherwise.

They had a long drive back to Thorp. "I'll always be your friend," he said quietly, and reached out and switched on the radio again. "Settle back and relax. Music calms the savage in all of us."

It was a strange comment, but Jessie was afraid to ask for clarification. There were depths to Hank that contained dark and troubled feelings.

And she couldn't fault him for it, not when she was in such dire emotional straits herself.

Six

Before they got back to town, they were talking again. Jessie asked about mutual friends and Hank filled her in. Neither of them referred to their kiss at the river by hint or innuendo, but it was there in the car with them, riding along like a third person. Like an intruder.

Hank thought about asking Jessie to have dinner with him at Merrill's, then discarded the idea. He was as disturbed about that flare of passion between them as he knew she was, and they had spent enough time together for one Sunday. He wanted a little breathing room, some time to figure out what was happening with them.

When they reached Thorp, he drove directly to the Shroeder house and parked at the curb. Jessie offered a smile. "Thank you, Hank. I enjoyed..." She stopped, uncertain of how to phrase her thanks, then tried again. "It was nice of you to give up your Sunday afternoon for me."

The remark hit him wrong, as if she honestly felt it was some kind of hardship to spend an afternoon with her. A cold, hard knot of anger suddenly weighted his stomach.

There was no one but Jessie to direct it at, and it was tough to remember his high-minded phrases about friends and friendship. When had she become such a martyr?

"Let's get one thing straight," he said curtly. "I didn't *give up* anything today. I did exactly what I wanted to do, take you for a drive."

His tone shook Jessie. Somewhere in this more mature, completely confident man was the Hank Farrell she remembered. She had seen him at different times today, and felt him during that kiss. But right at the moment, he was nowhere in sight.

She had learned to apologize, to appease and to do it quickly. "I didn't mean to suggest otherwise."

"No? That's sure what it sounded like." Hank was staring at her, and the harsh glint in his eyes faded as he realized that she seemed to be shrinking. He sighed miserably. "Jessie, where in hell did you get the idea that you don't deserve a man's attention?"

She nervously cleared her throat. "You're making too much out of a simple thank you. That's all I meant."

They could argue semantics until hell froze over and still be miles apart on understanding each other's remarks. Which was one big, fat, unfathomable change in their previous relationship. There had been times, some of them permanently etched in Hank's brain, where one of them had almost read the other's mind.

It was Jessie's fault that he couldn't see beyond her eyes and the guarded expression on her face. He had tried to be as open as any person could be with another, but she wasn't having any of it. The only time they had really communicated was during that kiss.

Frustration nearly swamped Hank for a bitter moment. Then he got himself together. Whatever he was undergoing, he couldn't ignore the sense of desolation he was picking up from Jessie. "I'm going to be busy for the next few days, but I'd like to set something up for Wednesday."

Jessie wanted to shout, "Why?" Why, when Hank was so obviously on edge over the two of them, did he want to see

her again? He offered friendship, then retreated, offered it
again, then became angry over a completely innocuous remark. Did she need this now? Did she need *him?*

Every drop of dissension stayed locked deep within her.
Apparently, she needed whatever Hank was willing to give
her. "Wednesday will be fine," she agreed in a tiny, unassuming voice.

"I'll call you." He started to open his door, intending to
see her to the house.

"Please, no," Jessie requested with almost breathless urgency. She jumped out of the car. "Bye."

Hank watched her go through the Shroeders' iron gate.
His jaw clenched. One of these days, he would walk her to
the door. One of these days he would . . .

He would what? Hank drove home questioning his sanity. By the time he pulled into his driveway, he was back to
questioning Jessie's secrecy. And her nervousness, her
weight loss, her air of fragility.

And when he took a soak in the hot tub after a bowl of
soup that night, he questioned the power of sex and why he
wanted Jessie when he'd be so much better off with one of
a number of other women.

Jessie's Sunday evening was spent in front of the living
room television set, although she absorbed very little of the
movie going on before her eyes. Dinner had been ready
when she returned. Bob had put a turkey breast on the bar-
becue, prepared a large salad and steamed some broccoli.
Guilty because she had left him with the chore of cooking,
Jessie had tried to apologize.

Thinking about the incident while she blankly stared at
the TV, Jessie knew very well that Bob's coolness had been
because she'd been with Hank, not because she'd been absent all afternoon. Sometimes, with Bob, she felt like a
wayward child, she realized unhappily.

And, Lord help her, she was so far from being a
child...so terribly far. If only she could tell Bob, if only she
could open her mouth and let everything spill out.

A tear seeped from the corner of Jessie's eye, and she put her head back with a dejected sigh, forgetting the scenes flashing on the television set. Hank replaced Bob in her mind. The day with him had been a strange mixture of successes and failures. If he really just wanted friendship, why had he kissed her?

And if friendship was all she wanted from him, why had she kissed him back? Where had all that response come from? She would have sworn she was sensually dead. Thinking rationally, she knew that the last thing she wanted was to become involved with anyone. Friendship, yes. But anything else was beyond her emotional capabilities.

Hank knew it, too. He might not have an inkling as to its reason or cause, but he knew darned well she wasn't purposely receptive to a sexual, male-female relationship.

Gunshots from the movie brought Jessie's head up. The next scene depicted two men, one of them bleeding from a shoulder wound, trying to destroy each other with their fists. A frisson of ice darted through Jessie's system and she got up and switched the set off. She abhorred violence in any form, and there was too much of it on TV. Sex, too. Violence and sex. Sometimes she could barely stand the thought of either one.

It was only after she was in bed that she stopped to wonder why Hank's touch didn't seem to remind her of that fact. Not that she associated Hank with violence. His youthfully exuberant fistfights years ago could hardly be categorized as violent, not when they usually ended up with laughter and slaps on the back from his opponent.

But sex was another matter. Why did kissing Hank seem far removed from the darker side of human sexuality? Why did she feel personally threatened at too much familiarity in a movie, or even at the thought of sex, and then respond to a kiss that had been unquestionably sexual?

That question continued to plague Jessie during the following two days. But she was busy most of the time and allowed it to really surface only once in a while. She went to the drugstore and filled Ann's shopping list, which included a notation for "lots of romance novels." Another drive to town entailed buying soft yarn in pastel colors so Ann could do some knitting for the baby.

Ann had callers, and it was usually Jessie who answered the door and escorted them to the master suite. Some of the visitors were old friends of hers, too, so she would join the women and sip tea or lemonade...and dodge questions about herself.

Along with the subject of Hank, Jessie had lots to think about. That desire to make a permanent move back to Wyoming kept gnawing at her. She mentioned it to Ann when they were alone on Tuesday, presenting it casually, as though the idea was of little import. After Hank's strange reaction, Jessie was a bit leery of candor on the matter.

Ann appeared delighted. "Jessie! That's a wonderful idea!"

"It's only a thought," Jessie cautioned, although she was extremely pleased at Ann's response.

"A very good one," Ann insisted, positively beaming with excitement. "Have you told Bob?"

"No. I—I'm not ready to tell Bob."

Ann's smile softened into a plea. "Please don't look at Bob's concern as interference. He loves you, Jessie."

"I love him, too," Jessie replied evenly. "There are just some subjects we don't agree on."

"Hank Farrell."

"Well...yes."

The expression on Ann's pretty face became very circumspect. "Bob does seem very opposed to Hank."

"He doesn't even know Hank. They've both lived in Thorp all of their lives, and from what I can tell, neither one of them ever made the slightest attempt to get past their old controversy."

"Then the blame is as much Hank's as Bob's," Ann said with a regretful sigh. "Men can be so stubborn sometimes."

Jessie couldn't help laughing. She was beginning to truly love her sister-in-law. Ann was a sensitive, caring person, and Bob was incredibly lucky to have such a wife.

Ann was lucky, too, Jessie immediately added. *Any* couple who had a happy marriage was lucky.

Later, Jessie amended that whole progression of thoughts. Luck had nothing to do with a happy marriage. Ann and Bob adored each other. They listened to each other's viewpoints and each of them respected the other's opinions. They talked and talked. Bob couldn't seem to do enough for his bedridden wife, and Ann was always sweetly thankful. The only place luck might have come into play with Bob and Ann was in their initial meeting. From then on, their relationship had been all their own doing.

Jessie's conclusion was chilling. She was still trying to believe Kelsy's most oft-repeated counsel. *It was not your fault, Jessie. You did not cause Allen's violence*.

But if Ann received only love and affection from *her* husband, why had Jessie received sneers and slaps? She had started her marriage with the same stars-in-her-eyes outlook as Ann had. She had been animated with happy anticipation, brimming with plans for her and Allen's future.

Her first slap had been because she had thought Allen was only teasing when he told her he didn't want her looking for a job. She had replied saucily, "Mr. Vaughn! Why do you think I got a degree to teach?"

The memory was too painful and Jessie ripped it from her mind. Then she grabbed the keys to Ann's car, told Mavis she was going for a drive and hurried out of the house. It was late afternoon and Bob would be home soon. Jessie had regressed to depression and it was her own fault. Comparing her marriage to someone else's, almost *anyone* else's, always lowered her spirits.

Mick drove off for the day, and Hank went upstairs to shower. He'd flown a charter for the Forest Service yesterday and another for a real estate agent today. Tomorrow, he was relatively free, and he was going to insist on taking Jessie for a copter ride. After his shower, he would find something to eat, take a soak in the hot tub and then go to bed early.

When he came back downstairs, though, Hank got a cold beer from the refrigerator and went outside. He was wearing clean jeans and nothing else. The descending sun was beginning to touch the tops of the distant mountains and he sat on the back porch to admire the sight.

Jessie, Jessie, he thought with a discordant sigh. She was never out of his mind, it seemed. Even while he was flying, Jessie was there. Her image was surrounded by questions and ambiguities, but it never completely left him. She was an ache he couldn't comfort, an itch he couldn't scratch, a thirst he couldn't quench.

And she was a constant, tormenting reminder of things he had tried so desperately to forget. It was all back and eating at him: the Shroeder's contempt, his own muleheaded refusal to see how Jessie's family was influencing her, and the final pain, the bone-jarring realization that her letters that winter had only been giving him fair warning.

The sound of a car broke into his thoughts. Hank got up and peered around the corner of the house to see who was coming. It took a few seconds to recognize Ann Shroeder's car and Jessie behind its wheel.

She was here, on her own, and it surprised him. Almost warily, Hank set the can of beer down on the floor, then left the porch. He was barefoot, and he walked only as far as the edge of the lawn. The car stopped on the graveled driveway. Jessie just sat there, not looking at him.

She knew Hank was there, but she hadn't planned to come to him, and she didn't know why she had. She had driven around, losing track of time, and seemed to be here without conscious thought. It suddenly seemed like a terrible imposition to just show up like this.

The engine was still running. Hank ducked his head to see her better and frowned at the abnormal pink color of her cheek. He couldn't tell if she was embarrassed, upset or what. "Jessie?"

She felt silly, about fourteen, and she took a deep breath. "Am I interrupting anything?"

Hank gave his head a shake. "Not a thing. I was sitting on the porch, watching the sun going down."

After turning off the ignition, Jessie got out of the car and walked toward Hank. Then, quite suddenly registering his state of undress, she stopped just short of the lawn. Hank's bare torso was long and distinctly muscled. Dark hair covered a triangular patch of his bronzed chest. His unbelted jeans rode low, revealing a tapering line of dark hair below his navel. His bare feet were long and narrow. He was masculine, handsome, sexy.

And she had no business noticing!

Spinning abruptly, Jessie started back to the car. Hank gave the gravel a dark look, then braved the sharp pebbles. "Jessie...ouch! Jessie...wait! Ouch, dammit!" He reached her just as she swung the car door open. Hoping his grasp conveyed a welcome, Hank took hold of her arm. "I think I just punctured the soles of my feet," he said solemnly.

"What?"

"Is there any blood on the gravel?"

Jessie's startled gaze went to the ground, and then she realized that Hank was only teasing her. She laughed, but briefly and rather weakly.

She seemed strung out, Hank observed. Even slightly disoriented. His heart went out to her. "Come sit on the porch with me, Jessie," he said very quietly. "Watch the sunset with me." He was still holding her arm, and he urged her toward the house. She stumbled, but allowed him to steer her across the lawn, up the porch steps and onto a chair. Hank leaned over and smiled gently. "How about a beer?

"Hold on," he added before she could answer. "I'll only be a second." Hurrying into the house, Hank grabbed a beer from the fridge and almost ran back outside.

Jessie hadn't moved. Hank hesitated at the door, contemplating her stiff posture, then walked over to her. He held out the can of beer. "Here, Jessie. Take it."

Her hand rose slowly. Hank quickly popped the top on the can and wished he had thought to bring her a glass. Jessie didn't seem to notice, though, and took a sip. "Thank you."

Moving his chair closer to hers, Hank retrieved his own can of beer and sat down. Jessie looked small, defenseless and frighteningly vulnerable. He wanted to know why, what had caused a mood that he'd seen once before, that first night he'd picked her up and brought her here.

But he also knew better than to ask. He took a swallow of beer and sat back, as though this were an ordinary evening and they were both relaxed and comfortable. "This is a nice time of day on a ranch," he said quietly. "The work is done until tomorrow, the animals are settling down for the night, everything is peaceful. I get a very real sense of security at this time of day."

Jessie's eyes narrowed, but she said nothing. She was facing Hank's backyard, showing him her profile. Beyond the lawn and a stretch of hard-packed earth, his outbuildings were becoming shadowy in the waning light. The sun seemed to be resting on the peaks of purplish mountains, miles and miles away, turning the western skyline to gold. It was a vista to calm anyone's soul, and Hank sensed that Jessie wasn't immune to its soothing beauty.

"I flew very close to those mountains today," Hank recited, keeping his voice low and in tune with the evening quiet. "My passengers were a real estate agent and a prospective buyer of three thousand acres of ranchland. I crisscrossed the property three or four times to give them a good aerial view, then set down so they could do a little on-the-ground checking."

He could tell that Jessie's body was losing tension. She was looking around with increasing interest. Hank was proud of what he had accomplished with the run-down ranch he had inherited. The kennels and the hangar for the helicopter had been added since Jessie had last seen the place, but every building, old or new, was painted and clean, the house included.

"What's that?" Jessie asked.

Hank saw where she was looking. "That's a hot tub." He grinned. "I like hot water."

"A whirlpool hot tub?"

"It's got lots of jets. Want to take a closer look?"

Jessie could see the bright blue cover on the circle of red-wood. "Do you use it often?"

"Almost every evening." Hank got to his feet. "Come on, take a look at it."

Rising, Jessie followed him down the stairs. The tub was located in the opposite direction of the driveway, on the lawn, so Hank didn't have to risk the tender soles of his bare feet to get there, she noted.

Hank had left his empty beer can on the porch, but Jessie carried hers. He drew the blue cover off the tub and laid it on the grass. The tub was about breast-high for Jessie, and she could hear the low hum of its filtering system. She dipped her free hand into the water. "What do you do with it during the winter?"

"I don't shut it down until it gets really cold."

"It must cost a fortune to heat when the temperature drops."

"It's my one extravagance."

Hank leaned against the tub and regarded Jessie. She was close enough to touch, and he was beginning to think about doing just that. Her white blouse looked almost luminous in the gathering twilight. Below it, she was wearing a pink-and-white floral-patterned skirt. Her pink-polished toe-nails peeked through the straps of white sandals. Her hair was slightly mussed, and her mouth was lipstick free.

She hadn't known she was coming here, Hank realized. She hadn't started out at the Shroeder's driveway thinking, "I'm going to see Hank." So what had brought her?

She was so pretty, so soft and feminine and pretty, and he couldn't stop looking at her.

The impact of his steady stare was beginning to interfere with her breathing. The evening and this place were very quiet. The loose ends she had arrived with weren't quite so pronounced now, but she was far from calm. Her insides seemed to be oozing together into a mass of rebellious heat. Nothing was settled in her life; there was nothing anywhere that was solid and comforting to hang on to.

Nothing except Hank.

She turned slightly, so that she was facing him. Her eyes roamed his face. She saw his pupils contract, his eyes take on speculation. She was confusing him, sending out signals he was afraid to act on.

"Are we alone?" she whispered.

The question hung in the air while Hank digested it. His heart began thudding. "Completely."

"And you're not expecting guests?"

He suddenly needed oxygen and gulped a lungful. He usually knew when a woman was issuing an invitation, but he was still afraid to trust his instincts with Jessie. Her moods were impossible to decode, and this one suggested intimacy. He didn't know if he should believe what seemed to be happening. "No one," he replied huskily.

She was troubling him, Jessie knew. But she couldn't seem to stop herself from drawing on Hank's strength. The tub had evenly spaced shelves around it and a set of stairs to climb into the water. She placed her can of beer on the closest shelf and moved very close to Hank. His warmth reached her, even without actual contact. "Please hold me," she whispered.

He swallowed hard, hesitated only a second, then put his arms around her. Hers locked around his waist, and her head nestled against his chest. Her breath seemed to sigh out of her, as though she had found sanctuary.

He knew he was much stronger than she. He was physically larger and emotionally hardier. And yet this wisp of a woman weakened his knees like nothing else ever could. Her hair smelled like flowers, and his lips moved in it while he drank in the scent. "You're trembling."

"I know."

"Can you tell me what's wrong?"

"I don't want to think. Just hold me, Hank."

Just hold her? When his every cell was suddenly burning with desire? When her smell was unmercifully arousing and the sensation of her small body against his felt like coming home? She was where she belonged, in his arms, and every protective instinct he possessed vowed to keep her there. To keep her safe.

Knowing that she had come to him when she was particularly troubled was deeply satisfying for Hank. It was what he had hoped to convey during their other meetings, that she would always have a friend to turn to, that she could come to him with anything.

But he wasn't feeling exactly friendly at the moment. He was torn up with ragged, raw, sexual need. His body was on automatic pilot, functioning without any assistance from his brain. He was hard and shaking with lust, a man in pain, a man racked with the knowledge that only this woman could completely relieve him. Only Jessie.

Just hold her? She knew as well as he did that he couldn't just hold her. That kiss on Sunday had been proof of that.

The tension in his arms relaxed so he could explore with his hands. He caressed her back, her small waist, the curves of her hips. And then he cupped her buttocks and brought her closer.

Jessie closed her eyes at the thrusting contact with his fly. She knew what making love with Hank was like. She remembered...or thought she did. Maybe it was the only real thing in this crazy world. She hadn't thought she would ever want a man again, but maybe this was what she had come to him for.

His mouth was searching, drifting over her hair. She could hear his overfast heartbeat in her ear, and her very bones seemed to be liquefying. Rising on tiptoe, she brought her arms up around his neck and pressed into him. Her head was back, her lips parted.

He could have her. Right now. Here or in the house. She was pliant and seductively female. She was warmth and passion and everything he had missed for eight years.

But he didn't kiss her. His voice sounded like a rusty hinge. "Do you know what you're doing?"

Her gaze strayed away from his. "Maybe I don't want to know."

His heart skipped a beat. That's what he'd been afraid of, that she was dazed and unhappy and reckless because she felt lost. "Not like this, Jessie," he said softly. Reaching to his own shoulders, he took her hands away and brought them down. "Denying I want you would be a lie, but not like this."

"Like what?" The anger in her own voice stunned Jessie, but the moment passed. She couldn't control it nor did she feel inclined to try.

"We're not going to make love when you're in this kind of mood."

She smirked bitterly and wrested her hands from his. Turning to the hot tub, she dangled both hands in the water. He was watching her closely, she knew, and she slanted a challenging look at him. "Would you mind if I used your tub?"

Dark emotions swirled in Hank. This wasn't over yet. Jessie's mood was confusing, but he sensed how tightly coiled she was. A good cry would probably relieve some of her tension, but she didn't seem on the verge of tears. She was daring him, taunting him, maybe because he was the only one handy.

And then, maybe she really was hurt because he had turned her down.

"Use the tub if you want to."

Jessie's eyes narrowed. "You think I won't."

"Do you want to fight? Is that why you came here tonight?"

She tossed her head. "You'd probably back down from that, too. You've changed, Hank. I remember a time when you wouldn't have backed down from anything, certainly not a chance to take me to bed."

"You've changed, too, Jessie."

"So I have." Standing away from the side of the tub, Jessie began unbuttoning her blouse.

Hank watched her broodingly. If she went too far, she might get exactly what she'd wanted. Even though he doubted that she really knew what she wanted. But she wasn't just any woman, and how could she help knowing that? Principles could only hinder a man so much. If she undressed and got in that tub, could he stop himself from joining her?

The blouse was dropped to the grass. Her bra was a silky scrap of creamy cloth, molding around her small breasts. The pulsebeat in Hank's temples began to sound like a tom-tom in his head. "Be careful, Jessie," he cautioned in a hoarse undertone.

Her glowing dark eyes looked directly into his. "*You* be careful, Hank." Her skirt fluttered down her body and draped around her ankles.

He stared at the revealing panties she was wearing, cream-colored, too, sheer, provocative. She had pretty legs. Even thinner than they'd been, her legs were still nicely shaped. Her thighs, especially. How many nights had he lain awake and thought about her thighs?

His jeans were stretched to the breaking point. His nerves, too. A muscle jumped in his jaw, and his own heartbeat seemed to be smothering him. "You're making this awfully hard," he croaked.

She sent his fly a flippant glance. "So I see. Where's the switch to turn on the jets?"

He'd had enough. Advancing slowly, his expression a dark scowl, Hank muttered, "Have it your way, Jessie. But don't blame me after you come to your senses."

Seven

As though Hank wasn't even there, Jessie turned away, unhooked her bra and let it fall to the ground, pushed her panties down, stepped out of them and walked to the stairs. Her bravado caused both her heart and head to pound, but she seemed to be pushed from within, a strange urgency without choices.

She didn't look for Hank, but sensed his movements beyond the tub. As she lowered herself into the hot water, she heard the sound of a motor. The water began churning, slowly at first, then with increasing turbulence. Shaking suddenly, Jessie found the bench, which followed the circumference of the tub, and sank down onto it.

Not ever in her life had she done anything even close to what she had just pulled. Why was she taking her own frustrated resentment out on Hank? He hadn't caused her despondency today; she had done that herself.

The surface of the water was becoming indistinct from swirling steam. The evening air was getting darker; only a small arc of the setting sun was still above the mountain-tops.

Jessie still couldn't look at Hank, but she knew when he climbed into the tub. He sat down right next to her, his thigh nudging hers. She thought of apologizing, but a simple "I'm sorry" seemed so inadequate for her abominable behavior.

She closed her eyes when he put his arm around her shoulders and urged her body closer to his. Then he tipped her chin back with his other hand and very gently pressed his lips to hers.

The temperature of the water was no hotter than her suddenly flaming interior. "Oh, Hank," she whispered. Her mouth brushed his and she felt both caressed and caressing, so immutably connected to this man.

"What's wrong, Jessie?"

"Don't ask, please."

"You want something. Is it this?" His hand left her chin to cup her breast beneath the bubbling water.

She could still say no, she realized. If she did, he wouldn't pressure her, although if any woman deserved pressure from a man, it was her.

"I feel so...shameless," she whispered. His hand remained on her breast. The moving water was silky on her skin. She couldn't see into it. Below the bubbling surface, everything was heated sensation, Hank's slick body uniting with hers, his fingers teasing her nipple.

Hank knew they were going to make love. He could resist her only to a point, and common sense had vanished with her clothes. Besides, there were times in a person's life when physical communion with another human being was as necessary as breathing. Maybe that's what was driving Jessie this evening, a force of nature that went beyond the practiced concept of civilized behavior.

He was glad she had come to him. If all she needed was affection from a man, it was best that she received it from a man who cared about her. And he did care. Very much. *Too* much, probably. Her heartache was his heartache. Her unhappiness brought tears to his eyes. Her confusion muddled his thoughts. Her desire made him remember and yearn to possess.

"Wanting doesn't make you shameless," he murmured, pressing a tender kiss to her temple. His lips moved over her face. "Besides, there's nothing wrong with 'shameless,' not between you and me, Jessie."

Jessie's face was turned up to receive the kisses falling on her nose, her cheeks, her forehead. She began doing the same to him, dropping little kisses on whatever her lips touched, his chin, his jaw, the corners of his mouth. Her fingers explored the hair on his chest and the firm, solid muscles of his shoulders.

However soothing Hank's rebuttal was, she *did* feel shameless. Brazen, wanton, daring. Her nudity was shocking in itself; cuddling in a hot tub with a naked man was so far removed from anything she could have even imagined only a short time ago, Jessie couldn't assimilate the change in herself.

Of course, this naked man wasn't just *any* naked man. She didn't even like men. Eight ghastly years under Allen's domination had resulted in mistrust of the entire gender. Other than her brother, of course. But she felt differently about Hank, which she already knew and had been trying to understand.

It was something that would come to her, Jessie felt. In the dazing, dizzying rush of feelings she was undergoing at the moment, she really didn't care why Hank was different from other men. He just was.

"I need you," she whispered breathlessly, and twined her fingers into his hair, urging his mouth to hers.

He gave up on everything but Jessie, the wet, beautiful woman in his arms, in his hot tub. His mouth moved on hers with all of the pent-up hunger he had been attempting to deny. She was hungry, too. Their arms and legs tangled under the water. Making little gasping noises, she rubbed against him, delivering a slippery, thoroughly intoxicating sensation of ripe and willing femaleness.

Their kisses were short, interspersed with hasty gulps of air. The skyline was darkening, the bubbling water gave off steam, and Jessie felt as though she and Hank were alone together in some misty piece of heaven.

He lifted her to face him and brought her down on his lap. Automatically, she straddled his thighs. The length of his manhood throbbed between her legs and she pressed against it, her breasts against his chest, her arms around his neck.

His hands were everywhere, touching her, while the urgency of their kisses increased to the boiling point. They prolonged the sweet agony as long as they could, and then Hank moved her again, just enough to allow penetration.

She was trembling and looking to him for support, her face buried in the curve of his throat. "Be kind," she whispered, suddenly afraid that he would take his pleasure and leave her feeling alone and empty. He hadn't years ago, but she wasn't sure of anything anymore.

"It's all I could be with you, Jessie," he said gruffly. "Look at me."

Her head rose slowly. Their faces were an inch apart. Her hair was a riot of damp curls; his was mussed, wet. Their skin glistened with moisture. They were both hot and breathing hard, more from their intimacy than from the water.

He lifted his hips, forcing himself deeper into the velvety sheath of her body, and his eyes held hers, conveying emotion, pleasure, desire. There was memory on the path of their gazes, but there was something new, too. Something that had to do with time and its passing, with who they each were today.

The pleasure built, and still they stared at each other. They moved as one entity, smoothly, flowingly, slowly. They couldn't possibly disturb the water; it was rushing around, gurgling, bubbling with a life of its own.

"You're beautiful," Hank whispered.

"Not as beautiful as you are."

A faint smile touched his lips. "We won't debate that point right now."

"No." She bent her head for a kiss and slipped her tongue into his mouth. He reacted with a tighter embrace. Their rhythm broke stride. He thought of a hundred ways he would like to make love to her, and he was suddenly unable to keep this slow and easy. His thrusts went deeper, faster, with more force. He was sweating and trying to be kind, as she had asked, but he knew he wouldn't be able to control his body much longer.

"Jessie..." There was anguish in the word.

She was drowning in overwhelming pleasure and spoke hoarsely, fervently. "I'm with you. Don't stop."

"Baby...sweetheart..."

The world suddenly exploded for Jessie. Her body heaved and clutched at the delicious spasms. She clung to her lover, her redeemer, with adoration, with loving gratitude. "Hank, oh, Hank," she moaned, taking his final, hurried plunges, rocking with him while the heated bliss within her spread and spread.

And then, oddly, everything was almost ominously still. The water was no longer turbulent, the jets were no longer hissing with air pressure.

"The timer was set for twenty minutes," Hank murmured.

Twenty minutes. Such a short span of time for such earthshaking events. Jessie raised her head and looked into Hank's eyes. A slow smile curved his lips, and she smiled back.

"Stay here and I'll go in and get some towels," he said softly.

She nodded, but didn't move off his lap. Instead, she brushed a lock of wet hair back from his forehead. "You're a very special man, Hank." She couldn't tell him how special, not without bringing Allen into it. But she could see in Hank's eyes that he was catching on that sex hadn't been as good with her husband as it was for the two of them.

She also saw questions forming, and a self-protective urge brought her away from Hank and to the bench beside him.

"It's nearly dark," she murmured, casting a glance to the fading, silvery light on the western horizon.

She seemed to be retreating and Hank was afraid of her slipping away again. He wanted to dry her off and bring her to the house. He wanted her to stay the night, to lie in his arms, to whisper secrets and listen to hers in the dark, to talk about feelings today and those from the past. He wanted to awaken in the night and feel her beside him.

He took her face between his hands and kissed her lips. Then he looked at her and didn't know what to say. There had been love in their lovemaking, just as there had been years ago. But he was afraid of it, just as he *should* have been years ago.

"I'll get the towels." Standing up, Hank climbed over the side of the tub.

Jessie put her head back and looked at the stars. Some were barely perceptible, some were piercingly bright. In another hour, the sky would be a brilliant display.

She sighed with the most complete contentment she had experienced since . . . she couldn't remember when. Sexual frustration wasn't something one should take lightly, but in her case, she honestly hadn't seen any of her emotional disorder as sexually oriented.

Hank had reminded her that she was a woman, a fact she had totally forgotten. She had started her marriage with every hope of a good sexual relationship, but she had soon discovered that a woman did not respond at night to a man who had been cruel during the day. Sex with Allen had very quickly evolved into a painful chore, and she had been extremely thankful that he hadn't had a strong sex drive.

Still, in thinking about this evening again, it seemed strange that the buildup of events since her return to Thorp had concluded in a seduction of Hank Farrell. It really had been all her doing. Hank had tried to keep things cool between them, but she had been in such a weird mood.

She wasn't now. She felt wonderfully calm and relaxed. The anguish she had been living with seemed faraway and still fading. Envy had caused her despondency today, and she wasn't proud of feeling envious of Ann and Bob's good marriage. But at least she was able to recognize it and feel shame for it, and that certainly was a positive gain, wasn't it?

And coming to Hank had been a positive move, too, hadn't it? Kelsy Worth, her counselor, would no doubt applaud the first spurt of aggressiveness she had felt and acted upon in years.

Recalling Kelsy's keen objectivity, though, Jessie felt a surge of unease. Maybe Kelsy would say that she had used Hank. *Had* she used Hank?

The answer was an unwelcome intruder in the peace she had just been savoring. She had hurt Hank eight years ago, and it was very possible that she was still hurting him. She was becoming very self-centered, thinking only of herself, what *she* wanted, how badly *she* felt, *her* moods. What about Hank's feelings?

Her heart began a remorseful beat. Hank may have read something very important in her behavior tonight, something she hadn't intended at all. Regardless of momentary satisfaction, her life was still in a shambles. She couldn't even think about permanency with another man, *any* man, until she got her life together. If then.

Besides, there was a tremendous difference between twenty minutes of lovemaking and commitment. Who knew that better than she? Only another woman who had gone through what she had would ever understand how a man could lie and smile and deceive until he got what he'd probably wanted all along, a weaker person to dominate, to rule, to use and manipulate.

Jessie was deep in thought when Hank walked up. She was sitting so silently in the still water, he asked, "Are you all right?"

"Yes," she replied quickly. He stood on the stairs and held up a large white towel.

"Get out, honey. You're probably getting pruney."

That "honey" sounded rather possessive and unsettled Jessie even more. "I've got to get going," she said in a tone that was both nervous and a declaration of something highly important and awaiting her attention.

As she stepped over the rim of the tub, Hank folded the towel around her. "You don't have to hurry off," he rebutted.

Which was the God's truth. There wasn't a reason in the world to hurry off. Whatever time she returned to the house, there was a good chance of Bob asking her where she'd been and what she'd been doing, but the chance multiplied tenfold if she arrived looking like a drowned rat. Which strengthened a case for staying with Hank until her hair had dried.

On the other hand, she was tired of worrying about what Bob might think of her activities. She was tired of worrying about what *anyone* might think of her activities. Was that being selfish, too. There seemed to be such a fine line between self-centeredness and self-assurance. Where did one stop and the other begin?

Whether or not her most recent actions could be viewed as positive gains, Jessie knew that she felt a whole lot steadier than she had only a very short time ago. And she had Hank to thank for that.

But thanking him would be an insult. What she had to do was convince him that tonight had been wonderful but had no lasting meaning.

Hank helped her down the stairs with an arm around her waist. He had pulled on his jeans, but hadn't taken the time to dry off completely, and his hair still dripped water, and a few drops glistened on his torso.

"Come in the house," he invited.

"Yes, I'll dress in the house."

He was right, she *was* retreating. Regretful, too. He clamped his lips tightly together to keep from talking about it. Jessie was still a puzzle, and it was disappointing to realize that things were pretty much the same as they'd been.

Scooping her clothes off the grass on the way, Hank brought her to the house. Inside, he showed her to the downstairs bathroom, then went to the kitchen to wait for her. He didn't want to feel anger, but couldn't help it. He'd known better than to let things get this far with Jessie. He'd sworn to stay emotionally uninvolved.

The only problem with that oath was, he couldn't completely disassociate emotion from making love, not with Jessie. Apparently she could.

Cursing under his breath, Hank opened the refrigerator door and glared at the nearly vacant shelves. Deciding on scrambled eggs to fill the demanding cavity in his stomach, he reached for the egg carton.

Jessie had used a comb she found in a drawer in the bathroom. Dressed and with her hair reasonably controlled, she walked into the kitchen. Hank was standing at the stove with a spatula in his hand. He glanced at her. "Hungry?"

The eggs smelled good, but she wanted to go home. "No, thank you."

He shrugged and gave the scrambled eggs a stir.

Jessie stared at his broad, dark-skinned back. He hadn't bothered to find a shirt, although he had put on a pair of moccasins. "Hank?"

He showed her a lifted eyebrow. "What?"

She dampened her lips. "I don't want you to think..."

"Think what, Jessie?" he prodded when her voice trailed off. "Get it out. What is it that you're afraid I might be thinking?"

"You don't have to be so sarcastic."

"No? What should I be?" Hank turned off the burner, put down the spatula and walked over to Jessie. "Maybe you think I should be thankful. Is that it?"

Her cheeks were burning. "Don't be absurd."

"Don't be sarcastic, don't be absurd. You're a hard woman to please. Tell you what, honey. I'll try to be what you want me to be, if you'll just tell me what it is."

"I *thought* you were going to be my friend."

Hank's mouth twisted. "I think you took us out of the friends-only category tonight, don't you? And that's what's bugging me, Jessie. Not that we made love. I could never regret making love with you. But you're afraid of where it might lead, and *that* bugs the hell out of me!"

She swallowed, avoided his eyes for a moment, and then dared a brave look. "I think you're more concerned with where it might lead than I am."

"Or where it *won't* lead?" he questioned softly. "I'm still a fool where you're concerned, aren't I, Jessie? All you have to do to wrap me around your little finger is undo a button, or give me one of those soulful, pleading looks. How does it feel to know you have so much control over a man?"

The idea was staggering. She didn't want control over anyone. She despised the mere thought of one human being controlling another. It was what she had lived with for eight years and what she had finally escaped.

Hank meant a great deal to her. She hadn't come back to Thorp with that clearly in mind, but after seeing him again and responding to his kindness, to his offer of friendship, she knew she would sorely miss him should their relationship die a sudden death.

She was still warm and physically content from his beautiful, caring lovemaking, but her mind was in a state of misery. Tears filled her eyes and began to drip down her cheeks. "I'm so sorry," she whispered raggedly. "Hank, I don't want to keep hurting you. I shouldn't have come here tonight. I was so mixed up. I drove all over town, and then I was here. I don't even remember getting here.

"And I didn't plan to—to talk you into anything," she added sadly.

He was watching the emotional display on her face, afraid to trust it, afraid not to. "Are you sorry we made love?"

Her gaze dropped. "It would have been better for you if we hadn't."

His voice rose. "Better for you, too? Put my feelings aside for a moment, Jessie. How do *you* feel about it?"

She didn't feel shameless now. She felt embarrassed and ill-at-ease. But he wanted the truth, and out in the tub, while he'd been in the house getting the towel, she had thought it best to let him know that as moving as their lovemaking had been, it couldn't go anywhere. The truth was best for his sake.

"I don't want an affair," she said in a low voice.

"And you think I do?"

Her eyes jerked upward. "I didn't say that."

"You implied it."

"I did not! Stop twisting my words to suit yourself, Hank. I had about all of that I can take for one lifetime!"

His eyes narrowed. She wasn't referring to the two of them in that last statement, and that was the first defined complaint she'd made against her ex-husband. Maybe Vaughn had been an arrogant know-it-all. Maybe Jessie's opinion had counted for nothing.

She looked like hell, teary, pale and bedraggled. Instinct told him to let her walk out of here right now, to *encourage* a quick departure. But he couldn't do it. It just wasn't in him to brush past Jessie's very obvious distress.

Moving quickly, he pulled her into his arms with a husky, "Com'ere." He cradled her head against his chest and rocked her like a baby. She closed her eyes and absorbed the sensation of security Hank always gave her. His voice began to rumble beneath her ear. "I can't pretend you and I are like other couples. If we had just met, I don't know where we'd be. Maybe we wouldn't even like one another, although I doubt that. But we go back a long way, and I really loved you, Jessie."

She stiffened.

"I didn't say I still do, so don't get all tense and outraged," Hank cautioned.

Jessie pulled away from him. "Let's not talk anymore tonight." She started for the door.

Stunned, Hank watched her go. "You're a flaming coward, Jessie," he flung at her back.

She stopped and turned. "I never claimed to be anything else, Hank. Good night."

He followed her outside, off the porch and to her car. "We're not through, Jessie," he told her as he opened the door for her.

She sighed. "No, I don't suppose we are. In fact, Hank, I don't *want* us to be through. Regardless of my... recklessness tonight, I still want your friendship. But I advise you to think of yourself." Jessie's chin came up. She hoped that she would never be anything but exactly who she was for anyone again. That *was* a positive gain, and no one would ever convince her otherwise. "Can you accept me the way I am? That's what you said friends do for one another. Right now, I'm rootless and unstable. *Emotionally* unstable."

"Why? That's all I want to know, Jessie, why? People don't change without reason."

"I had a reason," she said with some bitterness. "But I'm not going to talk about it. If you never say hello to me again, I wouldn't hate you for it. All I'm saying is that my decision is to accept your friendship if you continue to offer it. Whether you offer it or not is *your* decision."

Hank stood there while she drove away, deeply shaken. He didn't know this Jessie. She wasn't the soft, malleable girl he'd loved before, and strangely, she didn't even seem to be the distraught woman who had returned to Thorp.

What did a man do about a woman who seemed to be changing before his very eyes?

Something was very different, Jessie thought on the way back to town. She felt so... was it free? How? Why? Was this sensation of breathing easier merely because she had made love tonight? Very satisfying, very pleasurable love?

She couldn't quite make the connection, but she knew she had crossed a line tonight. It was mystifying. She felt stronger, without those horrible knots in her stomach. She wasn't worried about facing Bob with wet hair, either. In fact, if he asked where she'd been, she would tell him the truth. She didn't have to explain herself to anyone, not to one single person on earth!

Kelsy had recited that very concept, repeatedly. *In your present divorced situation, Jessie, you are answerable to only your own conscience. When and if you marry again, if you fall in love again, offer what you want to give to your partner. But don't allow him to tell you what to think and what to do. You're an intelligent, capable adult. Don't let anyone convince you otherwise.*

She had tried to believe it, but this was the first time she really did. The very first time she truly felt it. She was not stupid or mentally deranged. The instability she had mentioned to Hank had more to do with her directionless stagnation than with emotion. She had to find a job and her own place to live. She would stay with Ann and Bob through the summer, as she had promised, but by the time their baby came, she wanted independence.

What a marvelous word. *Independence.*

It was a weapon, a shield, Jessie realized. If she were truly independent, no one would ever be able to hurt her again.

Why had it taken her so long to understand such a simple concept?

Eight

Jessie awoke very early the next morning. She had slept restlessly, having been disturbed again and again by inscrutable dreams of deep, dark water and chaotic confusion. Lying in bed, she tried to make heads or tails of the night, although Kelsy had advised her not to worry too much about dreams. *Everyone has an occasional nightmare, Jessie, and when one is going through a stressful period, as you are, you're bound to take your troubles to bed with you.*

But it was that very point that bothered Jessie this morning. Last night, she had snuggled down beneath the covers with hope instead of bad memories. She had lain awake for a while, concentrating on Thorp's possible employment opportunities, and, yes, Hank had been a big part of her thoughts. Luckily, Bob had been at some kind of meeting when she got home, so she had quickly showered and spent the remainder of the evening with Ann.

But that's why those dreams gave her a funny feeling. She hadn't taken despair to bed with her. She was certain things were coming together for her, but dreams like that made her uneasy, regardless of Kelsy's admonitions.

Maybe she had been restive because of Hank, Jessie speculated. Then, too, that thin line she'd tripped over, that one between self-centeredness and self-assurance, was still very obscure. She wanted to be adult about making love with Hank, and certainly about their relationship in general. But this morning, she wasn't quite so positive about that your-decision, my-decision business. If Hank took her literally, he might think she didn't care what he did, and that wasn't even remotely true.

Actually, she'd been insultingly cavalier with his friendship, now that she really thought about it.

Groaning, Jessie threw the covers back and got up. It appeared that she was getting very good at taking one step forward and then eliminating her own progress by taking two backward. If Hank decided to forget she even existed, it would be her own wretched fault!

Hank was up and already working when Mick arrived for the day. "Thought you were going to take it easy today," Mick called, walking from his pickup to where Hank was hammering a loose corral post back into place.

"'Morning, Mick." Hank gave the nail a final whack and straightened his back. "I was wondering if you'd mind handling the place by yourself for a few days."

Mick scratched the front of his shirt. "Sure, no problem. Got a long charter?"

"No." Hank gave his friend a wry smile. "I want to go fishing."

Mick never said a word, but it was all over his Irish face that he knew Hank needed to get off by himself for some reason or another. It was also apparent that he suspected the reason: Jessie. "Leave anytime you want to, Hank," he said generously.

"Thanks. I've got the truck all packed." Hank handed the hammer to Mick. "You know where I'll be if you need me."

"At Signal Creek."

"Right."

The two men started walking toward Hank's pickup. "Bring me home some trout."

"Will do." Hank climbed behind the wheel.

"Uh . . . Hank."

"Yeah?"

"If anyone should call . . ."

Hank's eyes became hard. Mick didn't have to spell it out; they both knew who he was referring to. "I don't think you have to worry about Jessie calling."

Mick nodded. "Did you put a message on the recorder for any calls that might come in after I leave for the day?"

"It's all taken care of. Just flip it on when you go." Hank started the pickup. "See you in a few days."

"Right. Don't worry about a thing."

Hank shook his head grimly. "I wish it were that easy."

At the kitchen table, Jessie was finishing up her breakfast. Mavis, who seemed in a remarkably bright mood, had insisted on making Jessie a ham-and-cheese omelet. "You're too skinny," the older woman had clucked, adding two slices of toast and a jar of strawberry preserves to the menu.

The omelet was delicious, and Jessie ate every bite of it. At least her appetite was getting back to normal, she thought with a sigh and a sip of coffee.

She eyed Mavis curiously. Bob and Ann's housekeeper was definitely not your basic personality kid, but she was actually humming while she puttered around the kitchen. "You're in good spirits this morning," Jessie commented.

Mavis smiled, took a look at Jessie's nearly empty coffee cup and brought the pot over to give her a refill. "My sister's daughter is getting married next month. A big affair. I can hardly wait."

"How nice."

"It's going to be grand," Mavis exclaimed proudly. "Carol—that's my niece—is a pretty little thing. She already has her dress picked out. Oh, my sister knows how to throw a proper wedding, I can tell you.''

Jessie smiled. ''Do your sister and niece live in Thorp?''

''They live in Denver, which is where I'll be heading next month for the big doings. I already talked to Bob about being gone a few days.'' Mavis's face lost some of its glow. ''Of course, I'm probably going to need another day off, too.''

''Oh?''

''To drive to Cheyenne to shop for a decent dress,'' Mavis declared with some disgust. ''I've looked the whole town over, and there's nothing fit to wear to a big wedding in all of Thorp.''

''All of Thorp'' consisted of Cleavers, a Western-wear store and one small shop that catered to the younger set. ''You checked Cleavers out? When I was in there last week, I saw a rack of nice dresses.''

Mavis snorted. ''Nothing good enough for my niece's wedding, I can tell you. I want something real pretty, Jessie. Something in a pale blue. Blue's my best color.''

Jessie looked the older woman over. The heavyset, bosomy woman's taste in clothing ran to practical, cotton housedresses. Mavis was hardly a fashionplate by any stretch of the imagination, but her desire for ''something real pretty'' to wear to the wedding was completely understandable. Jessie remembered her own mother going to Cheyenne for her better clothes. Thorp had never had a really good women's wear shop.

She sat back, suddenly alert. A women's clothing store, nothing large, just a nice little shop that carried tasteful— *and pretty*—things for mature women. Thorp's residents were limited, but there were a lot of ranchers in the area, all in all, a large enough population to support a good dress shop.

Jessie considered the possibility. She knew next to nothing about how one even got started in business. But what a lovely-to-ponder idea. She would have to check the town for locations, find out if there was any retail space for rent.

There were probably licenses or permits or some such fol-
derol to go through to open a shop, but Bob could no doubt
advise her about that.

Inventory was probably her biggest hurdle. How did one
go about stocking a shop? She certainly wouldn't want to
buy in quantity. It wouldn't do at all in a town this size to
have more than two or three of the same garment on her
racks. Even Cleavers adhered to that policy.

It would take some doing to get started, but it was certainly something to think about, Jessie decided.

For two days, Jessie tried to ignore the fact that Hank
hadn't called. Obviously, she had hurt him, and it stung her
ego to know how inept she was at conveying her thoughts
and intentions. It was terribly hard to communicate when
every word she said had to be measured. It was a little easier to do with Bob and Ann because her feelings for them
weren't blurred by the kind of personal slants she endured
around Hank.

And, of course, behaving the way she had the other night
was inexcusable. It was impossible to see luring Hank into
that hot tub as acceptable, no matter how maturely she tried
to view the incident. Some people could make love, enjoy it
and forget it. Hank wasn't one of them, which she should
have remembered from years ago. Jessie wondered about
herself, and had to admit, with a heavy sigh, that neither
was she. It was just that she had been in such a state, and
then, afterward, she had felt so gloriously free. She hadn't
conveyed her feelings at all well and had ended up alienating her best friend.

The whole thing was a sad commentary on her state of
mind. For Hank's sake, it was best that he had decided to
withdraw his friendship. In her case, though, there was a
hole as big as the Grand Canyon in her midsection.

She kept busy. There was usually some little thing she
could do for Ann, and when there wasn't, Jessie borrowed
her sister-in-law's car and did some investigating. It seemed
sensible to her to thoroughly know what her competition

would be before she got too involved in plans for a women's wear shop. With that in mind, she visited every store in Thorp that so much as hinted at stocking women's clothing.

Cleavers would be her biggest competitor, she realized at the conclusion of her quest. But because the small department store carried such a variety of items, it specialized in none. Its ladies' clothing section offered a smattering of lingerie, sportswear and rather ordinary dresses. One rack contained summer jackets, another, a few bathing suits. Toward the end of August, Jessie figured, the warm-weather items would be replaced with sweaters and probably one large influx of winter coats. As for the kind of dress Mavis was looking for, forget it.

Mavis was one-hundred-percent right. There wasn't one really attractive dress in all of Thorp. Not unless you were thirteen and into fluorescent colors. The Modernette, which blatantly advertised the age of its clientele with blaring rock music, was the busiest store in town. Giggling teenage girls were shopping, cracking gum along with their jokes and buying, buying, buying.

In her store, Jessie decided, she would have soft, soothing background music, a pastel decor, a coffee-and-tea bar and some strategically placed chairs.

Her store. It was becoming more distinct in her mind.

But so was Hank's silence. Between spurts of enthusiasm for her future, Jessie worried about Hank. Why had she been so abrupt with him? She had practically laid down an ultimatum, and the Hank Farrell she remembered didn't take kindly to ultimatums. Yes, he had mellowed during the past eight years, but he wasn't a man to jump just because someone should suggest it.

In the short time she'd been in Thorp, Jessie felt she had made quite a lot of emotional progress. Just having a possible plan in mind for the future was tremendous progress, considering her previous indirection. She was making mistakes with Hank, though. Her behavior was inconsistent, one time unassuming, the next time demanding. She was probably driving him crazy, especially with that insistence on intimacy he had done his best to avoid.

After her second afternoon of nosing through Thorp's business district Jessie returned to the house just before dinner. The next step in this venture, she felt, was to talk to her brother about it.

"Got a minute, Jessie?"

She looked up from the pad she had been writing on. Curled up at the end of the living room sofa, she had been attempting to estimate the cost of going into business. Her figures couldn't possibly be accurate, she knew, but she had, at least, compiled a list of common-sense items she would need: racks, hangers, a cash register, display cases and shelving.

"Oh, Bob. I want to talk to you, too."

He smiled warmly and sat at the other end of the sofa. "How are you? I've been so busy this week, we've hardly had a chance to say hello."

Jessie smiled, too. "You're a very busy man. I knew that when I came."

"Having you here with Ann during the day has been a tremendous help, Jessie. I hope you know how much I appreciate it."

"Of course, I do."

Bob was still wearing his business suit, although he had carried dinner trays up to the master suite and eaten with his wife. He reached into his inside coat pocket and brought out an envelope. "I received this today," he announced.

"Does it concern me?"

"It's from Allen."

Jessie felt herself go pale. "He wrote to you?" she whispered.

"He enclosed a letter for you, too." Bob extracted the contents of the envelope and Jessie could see a folded piece of paper and another smaller envelope. "Let me read aloud what he wrote to me."

She didn't want to listen, but she seemed to be frozen and unable to move.

"'Dear Bob. I know this letter will be a surprise. Please don't take it wrong. I'm deeply concerned about Jessie. Before she left California, she wouldn't talk to me on the telephone or agree to a meeting. Bob, I still love her and I'm worried sick about her. She isn't well. She has these flights of fancy sometimes. The divorce means nothing, a piece of paper. I want to take care of her. She will always be my wife. Please give her the enclosed letter and tell her how sorry I am for anything I might have unknowingly done to hurt her. And tell her I love her. Sincerely, Allen.'"

Bob held out the sealed envelope and Jessie stared at it as if it were a poisonous snake. "Aren't you going to take it?" Bob asked gently.

Her stunned gaze rose from the envelope to her brother's eyes. "He's . . . No, I don't want it," she whispered.

"He loves you."

She should tell Bob everything, right now and in no uncertain terms. Jessie opened her mouth to do so, but nothing came out. Her body burned with shame, renewed again by Allen's demented letter.

Bob was still holding the sealed envelope, but he had drawn his hand back. "What is Allen referring to, Jessie?" he asked softly. "What does he mean by 'flights of fancy'?"

Her mouth was numb and her heart was knocking against her rib cage. She felt guilty of something, convicted of something, and it wasn't true. Allen was the insane person, not her. But she had stayed with him for eight years, and she was still morally shattered by it. "Do you believe him?" she whispered shakily.

"I don't know what to believe. That's why I'm asking you about it."

"But you believe he loves me."

"Yes, I do. He sounds like a very wounded man, Jessie. If Ann left me—"

Jessie jumped up from the sofa. "Don't put yourself in his place! You're nothing like him!" she shouted, finally finding her voice in a burst of righteous outrage. She took a long, trembling breath. "I'm sorry. Yelling never solved anything. I prefer that you don't answer that letter. Will you abide by my wishes?"

Bob slowly got to his feet. "I'm not sure I agree with you, Jessie."

"It's not your place to agree *or* disagree."

"Isn't it? I'm your only family. Me and Ann, that is. Who else is there for you to look to for advice?"

Hank! Yes, Hank gave much better advice than Bob. With Hank she felt safe. Hank respected her sense of privacy. He . . . he truly cared about her.

Breathing hard, Jessie began to sidle toward the door. "Where are you going?" Bob asked with a frown.

"To—"

"Not to Hank Farrell, I hope. Jessie, sit down and talk to me. Tell me about your marriage. We've never discussed it. Your divorce, either. Tell me about it."

"Do not denigrate Hank," she said with so much breathlessness she wondered if she weren't on the verge of hyperventilation.

Bob looked down to the unopened letter in his hand. "You're not going to read it, are you? Do you think your attitude is fair, Jessie? I'm sure Allen made mistakes. People don't break up a marriage without a reason. But he is obviously very sorry. Don't you think you should at least read his letter?"

She was choking, barely able to draw breath. A band around her chest seemed to be getting tighter, squeezing harder. "Destroy it," she pleaded. "Burn it."

"Burn it! Jessie, you're being unreasonable. You're my sister and I love you, but I don't understand you. Deliberate unfairness isn't like you. You were always so pleasant, so cooperative. As a girl, you weighed matters. You respected and listened to our parents."

"Too much." Jessie was back to whispering. She had reached the living room doorway and was trembling, using the highly varnished woodwork as support.

"Not too much," Bob rebutted firmly. "How can a lovely, innocent young girl listen too much to the wisdom of her elders?"

"It wasn't always wisdom I heard."

"Are we going to debate our parents' intelligence? No, Jessie, you and I were never given bad advice. There were times when Father seemed rather stern, I admit, but family dignity and propriety were extremely important to him. To Mother, too. As an adult and head of my own family, I fully appreciate and concur with Father's strict adherence to propriety."

"Please don't lecture me." She couldn't abide lectures. Allen had reprimanded her smallest infraction with long, disciplinary lectures, and if she showed the slightest resistance to being treated like a naughty child, he would fly into a rage. No wonder she found it nearly impossible to express herself now. Eight years of withholding and guarding one's thoughts to avoid physical punishment was a harsh conditioner.

Jessie cringed when she saw Bob's reaction to her interpretation of his words. "My God, I'm not lecturing you!" he cried. He took an impatient breath, then waved Allen's letter. "I'm not destroying this, Jessie. When you settle down, ask me for it."

"Never," she whispered as Bob brushed past her and left the room. She heaved a ragged sob. She had thought— hoped—Allen was out of her life. But he was still there, infiltrating her family now, hovering just around the next corner. For what reason? She would never go back to him, never!

She had to talk to Hank. Even if she couldn't be explicit, just talking to him would calm her shattered nerves.

Weeping openly, Jessie stumbled across the room to the telephone. It was in her hand before she remembered that she didn't know Hank's number. The telephone book was in the desk, and she fumbled with the drawer, then with the book, finally locating "Farrell, Hank" in its pages.

His phone rang and rang. "Answer, please answer," she begged, then heard a click. "Hank?"

"This is Hank Farrell. I'm out of the area for a few days. Mick O'Dwyer is here during the day, but if you have a message that can't wait until morning, you may call Mick at 555-1633. Otherwise, leave your name and number after the tone and Mick will call you back tomorrow morning. Thanks."

Every drop of energy drained out of Jessie. Sick at heart, she slowly returned the phone to its cradle. Out of the area. When she needed Hank most, he was unreachable.

She walked around the living room, hugging herself, weeping silently. Where had he gone? How long was "a few days"? Maybe he had gone somewhere to get away from her.

No, he wouldn't do that. Not Hank.

Mick knew where he was! Jessie eyed the telephone again. She remembered Mick O'Dwyer as an old friend of Hank's, a buddy, one of the ready-for-anything bunch Hank had hung out with. Apparently he worked for Hank now, which Hank hadn't mentioned.

But then, there was a lot about Hank she didn't know. She was so focused on her own problems, she was aware of little else. But she was getting stronger... or she had been. Allen's letter was a blow she couldn't have anticipated. Even from a thousand miles away, he was trying to control her.

She had to see Hank, or at least talk to him on the telephone. If he was on a business trip, he was no doubt taking calls. There was no reason for Mick to keep Hank's whereabouts from her.

Wiping her eyes, Jessie returned to the desk and picked up the phone. A youthful, girlish voice answered Mick's number.

"This is Jessie Vau—Shroeder. Jessie Shroeder. May I speak to Mick, please?"

"Just a minute, please. Daddy...it's for you!" the child yelled.

While Jessie waited for Mick to come on the line, she picked up sounds from the O'Dwyer household, warm voices and laughter. Mick got married, she thought. And he and his wife have children.

"Hello?"

"Hello, Mick. This is Jessie Shroeder. You might not remember me, but—"

"I remember."

The tone of his voice didn't invite small talk. He would have no reason for shortness with her, other than Hank, and she wondered if Hank had discussed her with him. It was highly likely...and would be more discomfiting than it was if she wasn't already so upset.

"Mick, I need to talk to Hank."

"He's not around."

"I know that. I called you because of the message on his recorder." Jessie was trying to speak normally, but the tears just kept coming. "Mick, please. You must know where he went."

"You're putting me in a bad spot."

"Did he ask you not to tell me where he is?"

"No, but he didn't say *to* tell you anything, either. Besides, you can't reach him by phone."

"I can't?" Jessie's legs suddenly gave out and she crumpled onto the desk chair. "Could I reach him by car?" she whispered.

"It's getting dark. You wouldn't want to drive out there by yourself after dark."

She might do anything to avoid lying in bed and thinking about that letter. "Tell me where he is, Mick. Please." She heard a heavy sigh containing exasperation and disapproval. Apparently, Mick believed she was a threat to Hank, which hurt but was no more than she, herself, had been battling with the last two days.

Only Hank could tell her to stay out of his life, however. "Tell me, Mick."

"Fine! But *you* tell Hank how you wheedled it out of me."

"I will."

"He's at Signal Creek."

Jessie searched her own mind. Signal Creek...Signal Creek. It was a familiar term, and yet she couldn't quite place it. And then it came to her. Signal Creek had been a favorite fishing and camping spot of Hank's. He took her there on one of their early dates, an afternoon when they had still been getting to know each other, when their dates had been innocent and lighthearted, when a stolen kiss had seemed like a monumental occasion.

"Thank you, Mick. I was only out there once, a long time ago. Would you please give me directions."

"You'd better write them down."

"Hold on." Looking around, Jessie spied the pad she'd been using on the floor by the sofa. It must have fallen when she got up. Setting the phone down, she went to get it.

Seeing her figures and notations was painful and she quickly flipped the page back. Hoping for a normal life was probably foolish, anyway. "All right," she said into the phone. "I have a pad and pencil."

The fire was banked, with only a few remaining coals glowing in the dark night. Overhead, the sky was overcast, promising rain. The gurgles of Signal Creek and the chirps of nocturnal insects were pleasant sounds. Flat on his back in his sleeping bag, Hank stared up at the gathering clouds.

He should go home in the morning. It wasn't like him to waste time like this. Two days of pretending interest in fishing were enough. What had he gained, if anything?

He had hoped some solitude would give him some answers. It hadn't. His guts still cramped when he thought about Jessie. Almost every memory was painful in one way or another. There were some from way back that made him think about how much he had loved her. He had, desperately, and he was worried about what was happening now.

Had he ever really gotten over her? He'd thought so. He remembered whole weeks passing in the past few years without him thinking about her.

But why hadn't he found someone else to love? Why wasn't he married with kids like Mick and so many of his other friends?

Maybe what bothered him most about the present Jessie was how different she was from the girl in his memories. That girl had sparkled with quiet wit and a love of life. She had been soft and...

Hank frowned at the terms forming in his mind. Yielding? Persuadable? Pliant? Torn between her parents' wishes and his determination? He had pressured Jessie, and so had her parents. She had been caught between attitudes, his and the Shroeders'. He had coaxed her into some defiance, but in the end, the Shroeders had won.

Maybe that was why he wasn't able to pressure her now, because he had overdone it before and had lost. Was he hoping to win this time?

Win what?

Jessie saying she didn't want an affair was a laugh. What did she think she had started with that hot-tub seduction? He didn't know her. He didn't know what she was thinking or what she might say next.

But wanting her was becoming second nature...again. He was back to where he'd been before she left Thorp to get married: wanting, aching, consumed with the idea of sex. His own body constantly reminded him that he was a man. Why he should be so hung up on one skinny little woman with big, troubled eyes and an on-again, off-again personality was a painful puzzle. He was in lust, he thought wryly. Not in love, which was some comfort, but there was a danger of that, too, if he continued to see Jessie.

Hank drifted off to sleep contemplating Jessie's parting shot about their friendship being his decision. The thing was, that decision revolved a lot more around how she felt in his arms than it did around friendship. How did a man ignore a woman whom he couldn't stop seeing naked and dewy with mist, that he couldn't stop feeling, as clearly as if she were in this sleeping bag with him?

She had rode him with every eroticism in the book. She had needed him. *Him!* Not any other man. Him. Her hands, her breasts, her mouth...

Hank's thoughts floated into a dream, and he slept with a smile on his face.

Nine

An obtrusive sound woke Hank. His eyes opened. Immediately alert, he listened. A car.

Signal Creek was well off the beaten trail. He wasn't the only fisherman in the area who knew about this particular spot, but it was unusual for someone to show up in the middle of the night.

Locating the flashlight he kept handy, Hank shone it on his watch. Twelve-forty. He unzipped the sleeping bag and reached for his jeans.

The vehicle's headlights came into view, and he stood in the shadow of some big pines and watched them. The car was stopping beside his pickup before he recognized it in the dark: it was Ann Shroeder's car, the one Jessie had been driving around town.

For a second, Hank doubted his own eyesight. Jessie driving out here in the middle of the night was hard to believe. He resented her intrusion and the fact that she must have talked Mick into telling her where he was.

The engine was turned off and everything was quiet again. Hank stepped out of the shadows and picked up his shirt. Jessie got out of the car. "Hank?"

"I'm here." He sat on the sleeping bag to dress his feet. "What are you doing here?"

"It's so dark."

"Wait a minute and I'll bring a flashlight."

"It's going to rain."

Yanking on the second boot, Hank stood up. With the flashlight on, he walked over to Jessie. Deliberately, he directed the beam of light on her face. She turned her head quickly. "Don't."

He'd seen all he needed to. Her eyes were red and swollen. "What's wrong now?"

"I . . . needed to see you."

"And it couldn't wait until I got back?"

"You're angry I came."

He laughed without humor. "I'm surprised, Jessie. You drove for almost three hours, in the dark, with a storm threatening, and I can't imagine anything so bad that it couldn't wait another day. But then, how could I? Do you ever tell me what's really bothering you? Do I have the slightest inkling of what's going on in your head?"

Hank raked his already-tousled hair. "Do *you* even know what's going on in your head?"

"I'm sorry, Hank."

He groaned. "Dammit, don't apologize! Just tell me how you really feel for once."

"Maybe I *feel* apologetic!"

"Then why did you come? If you're sorry you did, why in hell did you come?"

Jessie swallowed a sob. "Something happened."

He studied her small form in the dark, keeping the light pointed at the ground. She had little courage, and yet she had driven clear out here in the dark on roads that were treacherous even in daylight.

He wasn't angry with her, Hank suddenly realized. He was angry with his own uncontrollable feelings and with circumstances. He was angry that she had so much power over him, and worried about how she might use it. Did she even know how close she had come to destroying him before, and that he was scared silly of it happening again?

Where Jessie was concerned, he had a soft center. Maybe a soft brain, too. Her slightest plea could wring him out. Her smile could lift him three feet off the ground, and making love with her sent him soaring into outer space.

"Come on," he said gruffly, and took her arm. Lighting their way, he led her over to his campsite. The fire pit contained nothing but cold, dead ashes, but he sat Jessie on a large, smooth rock beside it. "I'll build a fire," he told her.

Jessie huddled on the rock, hugging herself. The air was chilly and damp. She glanced up at the storm clouds, thankful that the impending rain had held off thus far. While Hank placed small chips of wood into the rough fire pit, she looked around his campsite and spotted the sleeping bag. "Don't you have a tent?"

"I like to sleep in the open."

"But it's going to rain."

"There's little danger of me melting. Besides, there's a camper shell on the pickup. If it got too bad at night, I'd move the sleeping bag inside."

A small blaze began flickering, and Hank added a little more wood. Jessie watched his profile brighten in the increasing firelight. His shirt was unbuttoned, his hair disheveled. "Were you sleeping?"

He gave her a wry glance. "At one in the morning? What else would I be doing?"

"Worrying, remembering, questioning," she said softly, introspectively. "Dreaming," she added after a moment and in a louder voice. "Were you dreaming, Hank?"

He carefully positioned two large chunks of wood on the fire, then stood up. "You might not want to hear about my dreams."

"Am I in them?" She laughed sharply. "I'm probably the star of your worst nightmares."

He didn't deny or agree with her conjecture. "You said something happened."

Jessie tensed. During the long, tedious and sometimes frightening drive, she had visualized telling Hank about the letter. But the reality of doing so was more difficult than she had supposed. If she could just be with him without explaining anything. Already, even though his welcome was hardly one to cherish, she felt safe again. There was something almost miraculous about being with Hank. She felt as though nothing could harm her in his presence.

She sighed. "Bob brought home a letter he received from Allen."

Hank's reaction was a perplexed frown. Was that what had brought her way out here? A letter to her brother from her ex-husband? "Does he want something?" Hank asked, merely because Jessie was obviously expecting some sort of response from him.

"Oh, he wants something," she said bitterly. "Me."

Fingers of ice walked up Hank's spine. "Who got the divorce, him or you?"

"I did."

"Did he fight it?"

"No." He wouldn't have dared fight it out in court, she could have added. She could have produced witnesses to his final abuse that would have, at the very least, damaged his reputation. And the one thing Allen protected was his public image. All of the Vaughns were like that.

For that matter, her own parents had been overly concerned with public opinion. Bob, too. It made Jessie sick to her stomach to look at Hank and remember the multitude of warnings, lectures and admonitions she had heard because of him.

Hank took a long breath. "I don't understand. Why does he want you now if he didn't want you then?"

"He's...erratic," Jessie replied, hoping Hank would accept that answer without digging further into it.

"Damn, it's starting to rain," he muttered, looking up at the sky. The chilling drops began to fall faster. They were in for a good soaking unless they got under cover. There was half of the night to get through, and if he was alone, he would head for the camper shell. Sharing that small space with Jessie made a disturbing picture, but sitting up in her car or the cab of the pickup for the rest of the night made little sense.

"Come on," he growled, and grabbed the sleeping bag, his pillow and the extra blanket he'd brought along. "Take the flashlight," he told Jessie.

They were already getting wet. The fire was sizzling and dying. Hank kept his food and supplies in the camper shell because of marauding animals, so he had to move a few things away from the door before they could climb in. Hurrying, he finally made space and then helped Jessie up onto the back of the pickup. She had to crouch to move around. With his height, he had to crouch even more.

While she held the flashlight, Hank opened the sleeping bag so they could both stretch out on it. "There's only one pillow," he said as he spread the blanket.

"And one blanket," she murmured. The interior of the shell was small and intimate, noisy from the deluge of battering rain. She felt Hank's presence in her very soul, and in her heart, which was speeding up and fluttering like a wild thing.

Hank was trying to look at this ironic twist of fate rationally, without much success. The idea of sharing a blanket and pillow with Jessie for five, six hours was both exciting and demoralizing. Lying next to her was bound to cause problems. He was already feeling her in his groin, and from the way she had said, "And one blanket," he suspected she was experiencing the same curling heat that he was.

He knew she had to be cold because he was. Outwardly. Skin-cold. Internally, he was plenty warm and getting warmer. "Get under the blanket," he told her while he twisted around to pull off his boots.

Jessie was glad to comply. She was shivering, and during the very few minutes it had taken them to gather up the sleeping gear and flashlight and dash to the pickup, her white sweatshirt and jeans had absorbed a lot of rain. She kicked off her shoes and slid beneath the blanket. It felt good, and she snuggled into its warmth.

To her surprise, Hank just leaned his back against the side of the shell. "Aren't you cold?"

"I'm warming up."

She was silent a moment. "You're afraid of me, aren't you?"

He didn't know whether to laugh or cry. Especially when she said in a low, regretful tone, "I guess I don't blame you. I've never been anything but trouble for you."

The sad thing was, he couldn't refute her rueful lament. She *had* meant trouble for him, in one way or another, from the first time he'd noticed how pretty she was.

Jessie took a sadly resigned breath. "You can't sit up the rest of the night. Lie down, Hank. We're both fully clothed, and I promise to stay that way."

The camper shell was made of fiberglass, but the rain was striking it so hard, it sounded more like a tin tub. The insides of its several small windows were steaming up. He could make out the oval of Jessie's face and her shape under the blanket in the dark, but that was about it. He felt oddly unattached, connected to nothing real or solid, and uncomfortably alone.

He didn't have to be. Jessie was no more than two feet away. If they both kept their clothes on, they could probably make it through the night without another memory to tear him apart.

And if they didn't, was one more memory really that unbearable? Besides, his body was charged with sexual energy. Pretending nonchalance with Jessie was impossible.

"Come on, Hank," she said quietly. "We're not children. Coming out here was an impulse I probably shouldn't have followed, but if you sit up all night, I'll feel guiltier than I already do about it."

Conceding her every point, Hank crawled under the blanket. They both tried to find comfortable positions without touching the other. "I don't need to use the pillow," Jessie offered.

"I don't need it, either. You take it."

"No, you take it."

"Jessie, take the damn pillow!"

"All right, fine! You don't have to get mad."

A long silence stretched. "It's raining hard," Jessie murmured.

"Pouring."

"I'm glad it didn't start before I got here."

"You were lucky. That road is bad enough dry." Hank turned to his side, facing her. "Why did that letter upset you so much?"

Her breath caught. "Because I don't want any more to do with Allen, and Bob doesn't understand that. I know he hopes we'll get back together."

Something raw and searing darted through Hank. "That doesn't make any sense," he mumbled. "Why would you divorce the man if you had any feelings left for him." He hesitated. "Jessie, *do* you have any feelings for him?"

"Nothing pleasant," she whispered, suddenly facing the fear in her heart. She wasn't even sure she hated Allen; she was just so afraid of him. And he was a clever man. Using her own brother to get to her was a perfect example of the way his fiendishly clever mind worked.

She was chilled again, icy cold and frightened. She looked toward Hank. He was so close and she wanted him to be closer. He radiated heat and strength and every good trait a man could have. Why had she been so stupidly subservient to her family's demands years ago? If she had married Hank, they might be like Mick now, settled, with children, with happy noises going over the telephone to callers.

"I promised to keep my clothes on," she whispered. "But did I promise not to touch you? Hank, the only time I feel safe is when I'm with you."

"Safe from what, Jessie?"

"May I move closer?"

"Aw, hell," he muttered. "Yeah, move closer. Do any damned thing you want. I'm putty in your hands and we both know it."

Tears struck her hard and fast. She sat up, unthinkingly pulling the blanket with her. Hank closed his eyes with a sigh of exasperation. "I'm sorry," he finally said. "Lie down. You're letting the cold in." He held the blanket up, inviting her to lie next to him.

Jessie was so mixed up, she wished she were dead. Kelsy had warned her against such depressing thoughts, but, dear God, was she ever going to do something right? Something she was proud of? Something that meant happiness for her and the people around her?

"I just keep making mistakes with you," she said on a sob. "I know I've been thinking of only myself, and I know that it hurts you. But tonight, when Bob read that letter to me, all I could think of was you. Seeing you, being with you."

He didn't love her, he *couldn't!* Even without their past, what kind of idiot would fall in love with a woman who moved from one crisis to another with the same regularity that most people brushed their teeth?

"Lie down," he said quietly but firmly. When she obeyed, he nestled her up against him, with his arms around her and her head on his shoulder. Instant desire flamed in his body. It took only the barest contact with Jessie to turn him on, and in all honesty, it happened too often from mere thoughts.

He forced his hands to stay uninvolved, to remain reasonably still. Her sobs stopped almost at once, as though she no longer had any reason to cry. Maybe he was the one who should be crying, Hank thought wryly. Jessie, apparently, had found what she'd been looking for when she'd driven out here, while he was suffering the agonies of the damned!

It's only lust, he told himself. Only chemistry. Nothing important. Nothing lasting. He wouldn't be permanently injured by a night under the same blanket, nor would she.

She moved a little, snuggling closer. "Lie still," he growled.

"Sorry."

His voice became cynical. "I'll just bet you are." At her sharp intake of air, he added, "And if you start crying again, I swear I'll..."

He was aroused and angry about it, Jessie suspected. She felt so bad for Hank. She couldn't help turning to him when she was upset, leaning on him, and she wished there was some way to make it up to him. "Don't be angry," she whispered.

"I'm not angry."

"Yes, you are. Talk to me, Hank."

"Go to sleep."

How? It wasn't possible to sleep with him wrapped around her. "I'm not sure I can."

"Try."

She squeezed her eyes shut, but that made the sensation stronger and she quickly opened them again. Lying there, trying not to squirm, she listened to Hank's heavy breathing. He wasn't going to fall asleep, either. She began to think about making love with him. How could she not? Beneath the blanket, their bodies were giving off heat and much more. Tangled together as they were, she felt his chest, his legs, the front of his jeans. His masculinity was like a cloak around them, affecting the very air they were breathing.

Would it be terrible for her to make the first move again? She suspected that he wouldn't, that he was trying very hard to fight the inevitable. Neither of them could ignore what was steaming up those little windows even more than the cold rain washing their outsides—desire, strong, pure, sexual desire.

Why did she feel this way with Hank? Why had she *always* felt this way with Hank? And why, in all that was holy, had she thought it hadn't mattered and married Allen?

"Do you remember the first time we made love?" she whispered.

"Jessie, for God's sake—"

"Do you?"

"No."

"You're lying."

"I'm *trying* to sleep." He turned over, quickly, abruptly, leaving her nothing but his back.

Jessie sighed and stared up at the low ceiling of the shell. She could raise a hand and touch it, if she wanted to.

She would rather touch Hank. Maybe she loved him. Maybe some part of her had never *stopped* loving him. He didn't seem to like her very much right now, but that was understandable. All she brought him was troubles and tears. Had she laughed once in his presence since her return, a real, genuinely spontaneous laugh?

Jessie sighed. Had she genuinely laughed with anyone in ages? Maybe with Ann, once or twice. But it was so rare when she saw anything funny about life.

"You used to make me laugh, Hank. Do you remember *that?*"

"Yes, I remember that."

Smiling, Jessie curled around him, pressing herself to his back. She curved one arm under her head and slipped the other around his waist. It landed just below his belt buckle and she left it there.

He guessed what she was doing and allowed it with a crazy, wild heartbeat and a hot, surging pleasure. She was the most baffling, perplexing woman in the world, one minute apologizing for bothering him, the next, seducing him.

He felt her fingers undoing his belt, then locating the tab of his zipper. "Be sure you know what you're doing," he cautioned.

"You make me feel so many things, Hank. I thought I would never feel again, but I do. With you." She slowly drew the tab of his zipper down. And then she had him out of his jeans, holding him, stroking him.

Why had he even tried? he wondered with a strange weariness, one that was heavily tinged with overwhelming desire. Jessie could switch moods at the drop of a hat, and he already knew how determined she was if she set her heart on something.

Well, this was the one thing he couldn't fight. It didn't matter if it was right or wrong, stupid or the smartest thing any man could do. When a woman did this to a man, there was no turning back.

He flopped over and brought her on top of him in one hungry movement. The fishing trip had been a waste of time and energy. Jessie was an intrusion in his life and he might as well stop kidding himself. She was an intrusion he wanted.

His lips took hers in a rough, needful kiss. His tongue plunged into her mouth. His hands roamed her back, her behind, her thighs. Jessie's heart was beating a mile a minute. She had excited him to a nearly savage embrace. The tension in his body engulfed her.

But there was no fear in her, nothing but the same wild yearning that Hank exuded. She tore at the panels of his shirt, separating them to reach his bare chest. He was already half-naked, and she wanted to complete the job.

"Undress," he growled.

"Yes." She sat up and yanked the sweatshirt over her head. Jeans were shed, underwear went, and then she was on top of him again, only with hot, bare skin against more hot, bare skin.

Their kisses landed with direction, their mouths open and searching. The camper shell was getting steamier, uncomfortably warm. Hank flipped a lock on the nearest window and pushed it open, letting in the scent of fresh, moist air.

They rolled over, putting Jessie on her back. His mouth moved down her body, lingering at her breasts, wetting them with hot, open-mouthed caresses. His tongue flicked against her nipples, sending spiraling thrills through her system. His hand trailed down her belly and stopped at the curls between her thighs.

He was breathing hard, conveying sexual turbulence. There was too much urgency between them for patience or restraint. When he found that she was wet and ready for him, he entered her in one possessive thrust.

Jessie's mouth opened for air. He was on her, in her, big and hard, and she had never needed anything more. He raised her hips and demanded participation, which wasn't necessary. She locked her legs around him and urged him deeper inside her body.

"Oh, Jessie," he moaned raggedly. There had never been another woman who could make him feel the way Jessie did, not in bed. And not in the back of a pickup, either. It scared the hell out of him.

While the rain rattled the camper shell, they made love, taking from the other, giving to the other. It didn't last long. They were both too breathlessly grasping for the final ecstasy to last very long.

Jessie swore she saw stars at that exquisite moment, and knew that the dampness in her eyes were tears of utter bliss. It took as long to cool down as it had to culminate their driving passion.

Hank took his weight off her by raising his upper body with his elbows. "You're something else, Jessie," he whispered. "How should I take you?"

"Exactly like you just did."

"I'm talking about—"

"I know what you're talking about. Be patient with me, my love. That's all I ask."

That "my love" had gone right through Hank. He moved to the sleeping bag and tucked the blanket around them. "Was I ever really your love, Jessie?"

"You were, if I remember the past correctly." Sighing, Jessie snuggled into the warm curve of his body. "I know I've been a trial, Hank. I know how much I hurt you when I married—" She couldn't say Allen's name.

Hank closed his eyes as a rebirth of pain arrowed through him. But he was also thinking of something else. "Are you on the Pill?"

Jessie stiffened slightly. "No."

"You could be pregnant right now. We should have used something."

A baby. She hadn't even thought about how careless they had been in the hot tub, and certainly nothing could have stopped them tonight. A slow smile curved Jessie's lips. A baby. Hank's baby.

"Would you marry me if I were?" she whispered.

Hank's heart skipped a beat. "I suppose we'd have to take it under consideration," he said carefully.

She laughed and heard the joy in it herself. She *could* still laugh. With Hank, she could. "You would marry me, wouldn't you? You're too honorable not to."

"Since when has Hank Farrell been honorable?" he drawled dryly.

"You always were. The problem was, I'm probably the only one who knew it."

"And yet you married someone else," Hank said softly.

Jessie's laughter died. "Do you think you will ever be able to forgive me?"

"Do you forgive yourself, Jessie? Your marriage didn't last. Ours would have. Have you ever thought about that?"

"Many times." Her voice was low, ashamed, remorseful.

Hank brought her closer. "Forget it. There's no point in beating a dead horse." He paused, then said, "If you would only talk about it with me."

"You just said—"

"I'm referring to your marriage."

Her voice got very small. "Why is that so important to you? What difference does it make what happened in a bad marriage? Knowing every single detail couldn't change the past."

"It's because there are eight missing years, Jessie. Eight years out of our lives. Why wouldn't I wonder? Reverse it. If it were me refusing to talk about something, wouldn't you wonder?"

"You've had girlfriends. Have I asked about them?"

"That's different. I didn't marry any of them."

"But . . . did you love any of them?"

Hank took a long breath. "No, I've only loved one woman, and it was a long time ago."

Jessie worked her arms up around his neck. "She loved you, too, Hank."

Tears burned his eyes. "Jessie, you really know how to wring me out."

"Make love to me," she whispered.

"It's going to be morning in a few hours. We better get some sleep."

"Later. Do it slowly this time."

Slowly. Yes. Slowly and deliberately. So far, in the two times they had made love, Jessie had been the aggressor. It was time she got a taste of *his* brand of seduction.

He began with a long, simmering kiss.

Ten

___

The sun was shining when Jessie opened her eyes. She was alone in the camper. The back door was open and warm, pine-scented air was drifting in. She could hear the buzzing of insects, some birdcalls. It was a beautiful, bright morning, and she stretched languorously, feeling very much like a cat who had just polished off a bowl of rich cream.

Her troubles seemed light-years away. Hank filled her mind, her soul, and she wanted to cling to the lovely feeling. Smiling, she stretched again. Her naked body bore the marks of the night's very thorough lovemaking, an ache here, a tender spot there. Hank's marks, she thought contentedly. She could happily go through life with Hank's marks on her.

Jessie's smile dimmed a fraction. As close as they'd been in the night, Hank had held something back. Even when they had been in another world and almost crazed with passion, he hadn't mentioned love. He'd said "I want you" in every way possible, but he had never said "I love you."

Had she said it? She had thought it, she knew, and it was entirely possible that the words had spilled out once or twice. But if they had and if Hank had heard them, he hadn't let on.

It was undoubtedly best if he hadn't heard her. Or had the good sense not to take her seriously. But if she really believed that, why was there a small empty spot in her heart? Did she want Hank to be in love with her? Did she want to be in love herself?

"Good morning."

Hank was peeking through one of the small windows. Jessie clutched the blanket around herself and smiled. "Good morning." He came around to the back of the pickup and sat on the tailgate at the opened door.

"Don't look at me," she begged, her hands going to her face. "I must look horrible."

"You couldn't."

Jessie's joy returned. With few words and a warm expression, Hank made everything all right. What a special man he was. Jessie noticed how crisply clean he was and that he had shaved. "What do you use for a bathtub around here?"

"The creek. But it's cold enough to turn your blood to ice, so you might want to heat some water and take a sponge bath."

"No, I'll use the creek, too."

"There's a clean towel in the box over there."

They had slept with boxes of food and supplies. "No wonder we didn't have much room," Jessie drawled, looking around the cramped quarters.

Hank grinned. "It beat drowning, didn't it?"

"It beat the Ritz," she said serenely. "It was a wonderful, wonderful night."

He stood up. "Yes, it was." Picking up a box, Hank walked away. "I'll start breakfast."

He was still holding something back, Jessie realized, biting her lip. Their lovemaking had been very meaningful and he wasn't completely comfortable about it. Could she blame him? He had given her everything eight years ago, and he was leery of risking his heart again. She was capable of understanding that. And she was just as leery as he was, so how did she even have the nerve to question Hank's attitude?

Dressing quickly, Jessie climbed out of the camper shell. She would have to put the same clothes back on after she bathed, but nothing was going to stop her from a refreshing dip in that creek. She was a little logy from the almost sleepless night, and a cold-water bath was exactly what she needed to wake up.

"Here," Hank said as she passed through the campsite. "Soap. And you can use my toothbrush."

"Thanks."

When she came back ten minutes later, Hank was forking crisp bacon out of a frying pan over the fire. Jessie felt clean, very wide awake and chilled to the bone. Any remnants of sleep had instantly disappeared in the freezing creek water.

She laid the bar of soap and Hank's toothbrush on top of the towel she placed on a patch of grass. "How long are you staying here?"

"I was thinking about leaving today." Hank cast her a brief glance, then turned back to the eggs he was cooking. "Does anyone know you're here?"

"I left a note."

"Good. At least your brother won't have the county mounties out looking for you." He grinned, but rather humorlessly. "On the other hand, if he knows you're with me, that's exactly what he might do."

"No," Jessie rebutted quietly, sitting on the same rock she had used last night. "Bob might be upset, but he wouldn't call the police just because I was with you."

"All night?" Hank reminded questioningly, a little sardonically.

"Well, I'm sure he won't like that, but do you want to know something, Hank? I really don't care. I'm sick of living my life to please other people."

He stood up slowly. "Do you really mean that?" He didn't like thinking in terms of Jessie having finally grown up, but he remembered so well how passively she had bent to her family's will. Apparently, from the hints she occasionally dropped about her marriage, she had done the same with her ex-husband.

Hank studied her fresh-faced appeal. Jessie didn't need a lot of gunk on her face to be pretty. Even during the worst of his bad times after she left Thorp, he had never stopped thinking of her as the prettiest girl he'd ever known. At her present weight, her face was more angular than it used to be, but her eyes were no longer dull, he saw with the gratifying warmth of true affection.

She flashed a brave smile. "I mean it."

Hank felt her determination, but he also heard a thread of uncertainty in her voice. Bob Shroeder was a strong personality to buck, and as the last of Jessie's family, his opinion was bound to carry a lot of weight.

It came to Hank, though, that whatever Jessie did, she had to do it herself. He could and would be there for her... for as long as she wanted or needed his support. But he couldn't make decisions for her or interfere in her and Bob's relationship.

As for him and Jessie, well, last night had been pretty darned telling. If she beckoned, he would respond; it was as simple as that. She was getting stronger. She had returned to Thorp saddened and miserably unhappy. The brighter light in her beautiful brown eyes now was proof enough of her growth. A day might come when she no longer needed Hank Farrell, and he had to be prepared for it.

Living on the edge, he thought wryly. His feelings weren't his to control; Jessie did that. His only safety lay in staying silent. Then, if she discarded him again—the word *discarded* caused an inward wince—he would at least have his pride intact.

"Hank, I've been thinking about opening a business."

He handed her a plate of bacon and eggs. "What kind of business?"

Making public her private thoughts was still a problem for Jessie. She became shy and unable to conceal her hope of approval. "A women's clothing shop. Nothing like the Modernette," she added hastily. "Clothing for mature women. Right now, if I wanted a good dress, I would have to leave the area to buy it."

His dark blue eyes moved over her. Even in jeans and a plain white sweatshirt, Jessie's good taste came through. Probably because everything else he'd seen her in had been attractive and becoming. Not that she leaned toward fancy clothes. She dressed simply, which he liked.

"I don't know anything about women's clothes, but you always look nice."

That sounded like approbation to Jessie and she beamed from it. Talking while she ate, she let her excitement show, giving Hank the dabs of information she had so far gathered. He ate and listened, acknowledging only to himself that Jessie *was* growing, even more than he had thought. She spoke freely, with animation.

With their plates empty, Hank set them in a pan of soapy water and filled two mugs with coffee. "It sounds like a good idea to me," he told her. "If there's anything I can do to help you get started, let me know."

Jessie's eyes took on circumspection. Hank saw more in their expression, a tiny note of sadness. "You're so good to me, Hank. No one has ever been so good."

He sipped from his mug, watching her over the rim. "Allen wasn't good to you?"

She stiffened right before his eyes. "Please, let's not talk about him."

"You brought him here last night, Jessie. That letter he wrote to Bob, remember?"

That abominable letter. She hadn't forgotten it, not by any means, but she was certainly guilty of an attempt to do so. Losing herself in Hank's arms last night had almost done it, too.

Every drop of Jessie's previous animation disappeared with the slumping of her shoulders. Was she ever going to stop using Hank? With every crisis, she ran to him for comfort. She teased him into intimacy, which in itself was shocking. When had she become so sensual, so focused on sex?

Dispiritedly, Jessie got up. "I'll do the dishes, then I better be getting back to town."

Hank set his cup down and went over to her. He didn't understand her moods, but his every instinct was attuned to them. Besides, he got as much out of touching Jessie as she did. Maybe more. Holding her, making love to her, was time without pain, without questions. With her in his arms, he could forget about those eight long years she wouldn't talk about and about the shadow that appeared in her eyes every time the subject came up.

He drew her close, wrapping his arms around her, his cheek lying on the top of her head. They had made love twice before dawn and once with the sun coming up. But holding her was arousing. It always had been, and he knew it always would be.

He was destined to love a troubled woman. Looking back, Jessie never had been an easy woman to love. If she hadn't been worried about her parents' opinion, she'd worried about someone else's. The town's in general, her brother's, her friends'. Maybe she was finally getting over that. For her sake, Hank truly hoped so.

That was one thing that had never bothered him, what anyone else might think about his activities. Nowadays, granted, he was a little more concerned about public opinion than he used to be. But it sure didn't influence every move he made, not by a long shot.

Hank felt her slender arms tighten around his waist. He might never completely understand Jessie, but a man didn't have to comprehend everything about a woman to want her.

He tipped her chin and kissed her mouth, slowly, lazily. His pulse rate picked up. They had reached some sort of plateau in their relationship, one on which they communicated perfectly. They were lovers, and gaining in emotional strength or not, Jessie was going to be his for a while yet.

His tongue dipped into her mouth as he gathered her up into a more needful embrace. His body was addicted to Jessie's, mindful of her every curve, her haunting, exquisite femaleness.

She hadn't expected this sort of sensual assault when he had put his arms around her, but she couldn't deny its power. Hank's kisses made her head spin, her breasts ache, her temperature soar. She had seduced him twice, which stunned her every time she thought about it, but he had wrested the role of seducer away from her last night. Once he had stopped fighting the chemistry between them, he had shown her just how overwhelming a man's desire could really be.

He was showing her again. His hands were hard and hot on her body, searing her skin through her clothing. His mouth possessed hers, demanding her affection, her participation.

Her response to such fervor was astonishing. She had awakened only a short time ago utterly replete, content from the roots of her hair to the tips of her toes. And here she was, straining against him, tingling, trembling, wanting.

"I don't want you to leave yet," he whispered between nipping, tugging kisses to her lips.

"Apparently." She was finding breathing an awful chore.

Hank's hands were under her sweatshirt, absorbing the sweet silk of her skin. He flicked the clasp of her bra, freeing her breasts, then undid the button at the waist of her jeans.

"It's broad daylight," she murmured, closing her eyes as he worked her zipper down.

"I've been here three days, and you're the only person I've seen."

"But someone *could* come along."

"Then they'll get an eyeful, won't they?" He wasn't smiling and it wasn't a joke. Almost grimly, Hank swept her up into his arms. Jessie might be trying not to live her life to appease others, but she hadn't quite made the grade yet. He didn't give a personal damn who might come along and catch a glimpse of them making love. It wasn't likely to happen, and if it did, the intruder wouldn't see much. The door of the camper was facing away from the road, and its windows were too small to give anyone much of a view from a distance.

Jessie hugged his neck during the short trip to the camper. If Hank wasn't worried about someone coming along, she wouldn't be, either, she decided in a burst of daring.

She nibbled on his ear, sending a spiky thrill through Hank's system. He set her on the tailgate of the pickup and stood back to unbutton his shirt.

"Let me," Jessie said huskily, reaching out to him. He stepped closer and watched her while she undid his buttons. Her cheeks were pink, her eyes glowing.

"You're beautiful, Jessie."

She smiled. "Right now I feel beautiful." Her eyes rose to his. "You make me feel beautiful." Parting the front of his shirt, she pressed her mouth to his chest. "What's happening to us, Hank?"

Was she asking for feelings? Did she dare ask for his soul when hers was so guarded? Maybe they should be talking about love right now. Maybe they were more than just lovers. Maybe, with their past, anything other than total and complete surrender to each other was a farce.

But he couldn't risk it. Not until Jessie opened up with him. The day she said "Hank, I want you to know everything that happened in the past eight years. I *need* to know," would be the day he'd start believing that something more than wild, uninhibited sex was possible between them.

He wove his fingers into her hair while he looked off into the distance with a sorrowful expression. "You know as much about it as I do, Jessie," he murmured gently, unable to hurt her at this moment with even the slightest reference to what he was thinking.

Bending his head then, cupping her face between his hands, he kissed her. The intensity of their emotions flared again. His thumbs caressed the smoothness of her cheeks, while he inhaled the clean, soap-scented smell of her.

As she had last night, Jessie thought of the first time they had made love. Hank had been so persistent in his pursuit. Little by little, date by date, he had conquered her fears, her sincere belief that a "nice" girl didn't go all the way, especially with a hotheaded young man her parents were so adamantly opposed to.

But Hank hadn't been only hotheaded; he'd also been hot-blooded. And he couldn't seem to kiss her enough, hold her enough, touch her enough. Their dates had evolved into little more than long petting sessions. He talked about love all the time, and marriage. And he never stopped kissing her. His caresses became bolder. They kept going farther, and farther.

And then one night, under a full moon and with the car radio playing soft music, kisses and caresses were no longer enough for her, either. She had looked at his nakedness and touched it with amazement. Feeling Hank's body pressed against hers through clothing had only given her an erotic hint of its strength and beauty.

She had become a woman that night, but only physically, she now realized. Emotionally, she had still been a child, steered and directed by her parents. For quite some time, she lived two lives. With Hank, she was an adult, with her family, she was a piece of clay, actually going along with their criticism of Hank, hiding her real feelings for him to maintain the facade of dignity the elder Shroeders demanded from their children.

And she'd chosen Allen because everyone thought he was so wonderful and she couldn't have Hank, anyway.

Lord what a waste. What a horrible, soul-sickening waste.

Jessie slipped from Hank's arms and drew her sweatshirt over her head. His eyes were smoky with desire. They shed their clothes quickly, urgently, and crawled into the camper shell.

Lying on her back, Jessie held her arms up. "Whatever else happened in our lives, you were my first love," she whispered raggedly.

His heart nearly stopped. He held her so tightly, he wondered if he might be smothering her. "And you were mine," he whispered hoarsely.

They were knocking down barriers, even without trying. Jessie began to sob quietly. "I loved you," she wept. "I loved you so much."

Tears filled his eyes. "I know, honey. I know."

"How you must have hated me when I—"

"Don't. I never hated you, never."

"You were hurt."

"Yes, I was hurt."

Jessie's arms tightened around his neck. "I'm never going to hurt you again." She swallowed her tears. "Hank, I mean that. If you want me to stay away from you, I will. I'm forever running to you with my problems, and I'm so sorry for it."

He raised his head, then wiped the tears away from beneath her eyes. "I don't want you to stay away from me. Jessie, who went looking for whom? When I heard you were back, I went nuts trying to stop myself from going to see you. I didn't even know you were divorced and I couldn't stop myself."

Through tear-blurred eyes, she absorbed the loving expression on his face. There was no comparison between Hank and Allen. How could one man be so cruel and another so kind? She had thought herself repulsed by men in general, but it wasn't true. It was a wonderful discovery and something to be passed on to other women who had gone through what she had.

She was progressing rapidly now, making career plans for the future, realizing that she was as entitled to happiness as anyone else. She probably would have eventually reached this stage all by herself, but certainly not as quickly as she had with Hank's support.

Closing her eyes, Jessie drew his head down. Their lips met in a beautiful kiss of complete and total oneness. There was time to talk about love, the rest of the summer, the winter, maybe even years. There was no reason to rush into anything. They didn't need explicit promises and avowals, not now. Not yet.

She would go forward with her plans for the store; Hank would continue with his own businesses. But they would see each other and become closer.

Their lovemaking was unhurried and deeply moving. Hank rested on his elbows and loved her slowly, watching her response on her face. He wouldn't allow thoughts of that still-secret, still-guarded part of her life to intrude on their new understanding. Just knowing that she had truly loved him before had opened a locked door. The past was scaling away, old hurts were diminishing.

He wouldn't talk about love now, but it was on her face and in his heart. He felt so protective of her, so lovingly possessive. Allen Vaughn could write all the letters he wanted and to anyone he wanted. But there was no doubt in Hank's mind that Jessie was forever through with her ex-husband. There was something satisfying in that, too. Whatever had caused the breakup had happened before her return to Thorp and without Hank's influence. As much as he hated her having been married to another man, it was good to know that he hadn't interfered.

"My own special Jessie," he said softly.

The endearing phrase saturated her senses. "You make me want so much," she whispered. "You give me hope... and confidence."

"We're good together, Jessie."

"Very good."

His eyes took on a smoldering expression as he executed a long, slow slide deep into her heat. "I might never get enough of you."

Her lips parted for a quick, urgent breath. The sensitivity of tender lovemaking was evolving into electrifying sexuality. Her heart, her soul belonged to this man. Why had she ever doubted it?

Their kisses became stormy, tormented, demanding. And their final ascent to completion was emotional enough for tears. They clung together long after the necessity to have each other's body passed.

Driving his pickup, Hank followed Jessie's car back to Thorp. They stopped a few miles out of town and got out of their vehicles. Standing beside Jessie's, Hank touched her hair in a sweetly possessive gesture, winding a strand around and around his forefinger. "I'd like to come over and talk to Bob, Jessie. It's time he and I got to know one another."

"It is time," she agreed quietly. "And I do want the two of you to get over that old trouble from the past. But I don't want to rush it, Hank. Bob and I have some things to work out, too. I'd like to get on a better footing with him myself before you get involved. Can you understand that?"

"Maybe it would help you if he got to know me better."

"Possibly." Jessie looked away from the hopeful light in his eyes. There was so much more to the situation than Hank knew. Than Bob knew, for that matter. She couldn't stay silent on the details of her marriage much longer. Not with Allen writing to her brother and Bob thinking she was unfair because she was so determinedly opposed to the contact.

Looking at Hank again, Jessie attempted to visualize telling *him* about her marriage. Inside, she felt the same, physically cringing from the picture. But Hank should know the truth, too. As emotionally far as she had come, how was she going to find the backbone to tell *anyone* that she had stayed with an abusive man for eight years? That she had lied and pretended and appeased and completely altered her personality out of fear?

Normal people didn't live that way. How would Bob understand it? How would Hank?

"Give me a little time," she said in a low, uncertain voice.

"I won't pressure you, Jessie. It was just a suggestion."

"One you were entitled to make."

Hank wasn't so sure about that. There was still something about Jessie that made any suggestion seem like pressure. He could see a lot more of her former self in her now, but there was still that one area of inscrutability. "Let's have dinner together."

Her expression cleared. "Yes. I'll meet you somewhere."

Hank nodded. "Fine. Why don't you come to my place around six?"

Jessie smiled teasingly. "Are you going to cook?"

"You don't think I can, do you?"

"You made a very fine breakfast."

He laughed. "So I did."

Standing on tiptoe, Jessie lifted her mouth to his, intending just a casual, goodbye-for-now kiss. But Hank caught her around the waist and gave her a real kiss. One that curled her toes. Breathless, she backed away and reached for the handle on her car door. "See you at six."

He closed the door behind her and bent down to peer into the opened window. "Maybe we'll take a soak in the hot tub after dinner."

"A soak?" she echoed archly.

"Or something."

She put on a seductive smile. "I'll count on that something."

"Do that."

Jessie drove away still smiling, but as she got closer to home, thoughts of Allen and confession returned. It was becoming imperative that Bob learn the true facts of her marriage. Hank, too. And Ann. Everyone would keep it in the family. No one else in Thorp would ever need to know.

But Hank and Bob and Ann were the very people that Jessie wished *didn't* have to know the truth. They were the people she could hardly bear the thought of telling.

If she was going to stay in Thorp, though, she had to do it.

Bob first, she decided, and the sooner the better. This afternoon, if possible. That way, she could talk to Hank tonight. She could call Bob's office from the house and find out if he had any free time this afternoon.

Yes, the idea of talking in his office was somehow less painful than a candid conversation at home. She would shower and change clothes, then call Bob. Ann couldn't be neglected, either. She would check on Ann and make sure she was all right.

By the time Jessie pulled into the Shroeder driveway, she was tense again. Would she really have the courage to recite the details of her marriage, not once, but twice today?

Parked and with the engine turned off, Jessie closed her eyes and breathed a silent prayer. It was immediately followed by conjecture. Maybe she should call Kelsy in Los Angeles and talk to her. Kelsy had the wonderful ability to bolster confidence in the people she counseled. She would be all for frankness, Jessie knew, recalling Kelsy's adamant attitude against bearing this kind of burden by oneself.

Jessie bowed her head and covered her face with her hands in a wave of pure agony. Could she really do it? Could she sit across Bob's desk and tell him how weak she had been? Was it even possible to convey her terror and how it had kept her helpless, dependent, subservient?

She had been an accomplice to Allen's violence. She had *allowed* it to go on. She had let him convince her that he wouldn't be angry with her if she didn't deserve it.

Now it all seemed so sad and utterly senseless. And she not only had to tell her brother about it, she had to tell Hank.

Dispiritedly, Jessie got out of the car and walked to the house. The day that had started out so wonderfully was rapidly deteriorating. The only times she felt any happiness at all were those with Hank.

And maybe tonight would destroy that. How could he not feel disgust for a woman who had lived the way she had for eight long years?

Eleven

The house seemed unusually silent to Jessie when she went in. A quick check of the first floor evidenced Mavis's absence. With a frown, Jessie peered up the stairs, wondering if Ann was all alone.

Deciding that Mavis had probably just gone somewhere on a short errand, Jessie climbed the stairs. She hesitated at the door to the master suite. If Ann was resting, she wouldn't want to disturb her, but she really did have a strong urge to make sure her sister-in-law was all right.

A low sound came from within the room, something between a moan and a call. Startled, questioning her own ears, Jessie quietly turned the knob and opened the door a crack. Ann was lying on her side, her back to the door.

"Jessie? Is that you?"

Ann's voice was faint, reedy, slightly breathless-sounding. Jessie's heart turned over with sudden dread. "Ann? Are you all right?" Quickly she walked around the bed and bent over her sister-in-law. Ann's face was flushed. "I'm glad you're home," she whispered.

"Are you ill?"

"I feel strange."

Anxiously Jessie sat on the edge of the bed and placed her hand on Ann's forehead. "You're a little warm. Do you have any pain?"

"Some cramping in my lower back. Nothing like I had with my miscarriages."

"Have you called Bob?"

"He's in court today, in Sheridan."

"Where's Mavis?"

"She wanted to go to Cheyenne to do some shopping. I felt fine this morning and told her to go ahead."

Jessie was shaken by Ann's appearance. Something was wrong, even if whatever it was had different symptoms than her miscarriages. She was in her seventh month, much further along than she had ever gotten with her previous pregnancies. This could be premature labor.

"Have you talked to your doctor, Ann?" she gently questioned, and saw a fearful glint appear in Ann's blue eyes.

"Oh, Jessie, do you think . . . ?"

"I only think we should play it safe. Are you spotting?"

"No."

Jessie got up and reached for the telephone. "I'm sure there's no cause for alarm, but I think I should speak to Dr. Haley."

Ann nodded silently. Jessie placed the call and gave her sister-in-law an encouraging smile during two rings. A woman answered with, "Dr. Haley's office."

"This is Ann Shroeder's sister-in-law. Would it be possible to speak to Dr. Haley?"

"He's with a patient right now. May he call you back?"

"Of course, but would you tell him that Ann is not feeling well?"

"Is she spotting or having contractions?"

"She's slightly feverish and has some cramping in her lower back."

"I'll have Dr. Haley call you in a very few minutes. You're with Ann now?"

"Yes. I'll be right here with her."

"And your name?"

"Jessie Shroeder."

"Thank you for calling, Jessie. It should only be a few minutes."

"Thank you." Jessie put the phone down. "Dr. Haley will call back right away," she told Ann with all the calmness she could muster. "Can I get you anything, Ann? Some fresh water, perhaps?"

"Nothing, Jessie." Ann's eyes contained a note of panic, but she tried to smile. "I'm so glad you're here."

"I should have been here before this. When did you start feeling badly?"

"About an hour ago. Jessie, please don't blame yourself. I'm the one who let Mavis leave. She's very anxious about finding the right dress for her niece's wedding."

"I know, but if I hadn't gone off last night . . ."

Ann lifted a hand from the bed. "Please stop. I won't have you reproaching yourself for this." Her lips curved in a sweet smile that immediately disappeared in a wince of discomfort. "There's another one of those cramps."

"In your back?"

"Yes."

Those "cramps" were coming with some regularity, Jessie suspected and glanced at the bedside clock to set the time in her mind. When she looked back at Ann, she saw the same realization in her eyes.

"Sit down and talk to me, Jessie," Ann murmured.

She should be calling Bob in Sheridan, Jessie thought, but was afraid to insist yet. If Dr. Haley showed the least bit of concern, though, she would use any means to contact her brother, court or no court.

Maintaining an unworried demeanor, Jessie pulled a chair close to the bed and sat down. The only topic she could think of to distract Ann was herself. "Did Bob show you the note I left last night? I taped it to the refrigerator so it wouldn't be missed."

"Bob brought it upstairs last night. You went to see Hank," Ann said softly.

"Did Bob mention the letter he received from Allen?"

"Yes, he did. Jessie, you needn't ever explain anything to me, but Bob is terribly confused about you and Hank."

Jessie sighed. "I know he is. But he always was. I was, too," she added with remorse creeping into her voice. *I never should have married Allen, never!*

"You're in love with Hank, aren't you?"

"I was. A long time ago." *You are now, too.* Jessie cleared her throat. "Hank and I haven't talked about love. He's been very kind and understanding since I came home."

"Bob would *like* to be understanding, Jessie. Ohhh . . ."

The telephone rang at the same moment Ann's face registered discomfort. Jessie grabbed the instrument. "Hello? Oh, Dr. Haley. Thank you for calling. . . . Yes, she's not feeling at all well. . . . Yes. Thank you."

Ann's uncomfortable tremor had passed. "That was a short conversation," she said, trying to quip.

"He's coming to see you, Ann."

"He's been very considerate during this pregnancy. Not too many doctors make house calls these days."

Jessie was positive that Ann's face was more flushed than before. But taking her sister-in-law's temperature or fussing over her could very well do more harm than good. The doctor was on his way and it seemed like a negative move to Jessie to let Ann know how worried she was.

Remembering her own goals for the day, Jessie put them aside and sat down again. "I've made a final decision about staying in Thorp," she announced quietly. "This part of the world is my home and I hope never to leave it again."

"Oh, Jessie, that's wonderful."

"I've been thinking about opening a women's clothing shop. Mavis talking about the lack of good clothing in the area gave me the idea."

"It's a terrific idea. Every woman I know wishes the town had better shopping facilities. Thorp is progressing, but not very quickly. You'll have the town's support, I'm sure."

Support instead of disapprobation. Of the two women, only Jessie fully understood how essential support was to a healthy state of mind. It was what Hank had been giving her, along with massive doses of affection.

But then, too, one could go overboard in seeking community and family sanction. That's what she had done before. Her parents had been wonderful people, but their choices hadn't always been best for her. As a girl and young woman, she had bent to their will with very little opposition.

Jessie wasn't looking for someone to blame for the past and truly felt that her mistakes had been her own doing. Although, she knew now, Hank, too, had made mistakes. His go-to-hell attitude had created resistance in more settled, prudent people. The Shroeders had seen him as dangerous, a threat to their daughter's happiness and way of life, and instead of allowing the older couple the opportunity to really know him, he had flaunted his unreserved individualism.

The pealing of the front door bell brought Jessie to her feet. "That must be Dr. Haley." Hurrying from the room and down the stairs, Jessie opened the door to the doctor.

Dr. Ralph Haley was with Ann about a quarter hour, during which time, Jessie wandered the first floor and worried. When she heard footsteps on the stairs, she waited on the landing with an anxious expression. "How is she?"

The doctor was a middle-aged, graying man with a naturally sober air. "She's resting now." Dr. Haley set his medical bag on the floor. "Ann said Bob is in Sheridan today. When he returns, would you see that he calls me? If it's past office hours, have him call me at home."

"Certainly. I was concerned about premature labor, Doctor."

Dr. Haley shook his head. "Ann's not in labor, but she is in the final trimester of her pregnancy and premature labor is a grave possibility."

"Should she be in the hospital?"

"I hesitate to hospitalize a patient unless it is absolutely necessary. Should she go full term, nearly three months of hospitalization would be very difficult for her. I want to discuss it with Bob."

"I understand." Jessie was hesitant about making suggestions on such a serious matter, but felt the doctor should know her feelings. "Dr. Haley, I came home this summer to be with Ann. I was away from the house last night and most of the morning. It won't happen again. I can personally guarantee that Ann will never be alone again."

The doctor nodded. "That's an important consideration. One alternative I'm planning to suggest to Bob is a nurse."

"Well, I'm far from qualified for that capacity. If Ann needs constant medical supervision, then a nurse should be brought in. But if you only want someone with her, I will be here."

"Excellent." Dr. Haley picked up his bag. "Have Bob call."

Jessie escorted him to the door. "I will, Doctor. And thank you for coming."

The day passed slowly for Jessie. Ann slept most of the time, relaxed from a mild sedative Dr. Haley had given her. At three, Bob called from Sheridan to check on his wife. Jessie explained the situation and told him, when he immediately became anxious, that Ann was fine now and that she would be with her every minute. "Dr. Haley wants you to call him when you get home."

"I'll do it now. Thanks for being there, Jessie."

Jessie heard the choked gratitude in her brother's voice and felt tears in her own eyes. This child was so important to Bob and Ann, as well it should be. But Ann's history of miscarriages made them almost afraid to hope. The room they had transformed into a nursery had been completed years ago, during Ann's first pregnancy. The door remained closed on that precious little room, and Jessie prayed that it would be needed in September.

"I'm sorry about last night, Bob," Jessie whispered brokenly.

"I'm sorry, too, Jessie. We'll talk about it again, okay?"

"Yes. But Ann and the baby are what's most important right now. I won't ever leave the house again without knowing someone will be with Ann. Please believe that."

"I do, Jessie, and thanks. Listen, I'll get home as soon as I can, but I'm up to my eyeballs right now. Tell Ann that I love her and will speed things up as much as possible."

"I will, Bob. And please don't worry. I'll handle things here."

Jessie called Hank at quarter to six and cancelled their plans for the evening. "I don't know what time Bob will get home," she said after reciting the events of the day.

Hank was disappointed, but understood Jessie's concern. "We'll do it tomorrow night. If there's anything I can do to help, don't hesitate to let me know."

Just the telephone connection to Hank gave Jessie that sense of security she had been deriving from him. He was so solid, so sure of his place in the world.

So different from the impression he had given her parents and most other people years ago. Bob still thought of him as a maverick, and while Hank was very definitely an individual, he was far from the rebel he'd been.

Strange as it seemed, Jessie realized she was in almost the same situation today with Bob and Hank as she had been with her parents and Hank years ago.

Only, now, she was different, too. Hank wasn't the only one who had changed.

"Tomorrow night," she agreed softly, counting very much on a long evening with Hank. She couldn't help thinking about making love with him. Their sexual communion was really the most beautiful thing that had ever happened to her. Even her memories of Hank's more youthful ardor and her own desire for him couldn't compare with their present involvement.

Her feelings for Hank were expanding with every contact, Jessie knew. She was probably deeply in love with him and merely reluctant to face it. To be complete, however, love couldn't be only one-sided. How, really, did Hank feel about her now?

After Jessie hung up, she warmed a bowl of Mavis's homemade vegetable soup, prepared a tray with crackers, fruit and milk, and carried it up to Ann.

Ann was far from vigorous. She ate, but with very little appetite. Jessie didn't want to appear overly concerned, but she couldn't help feeling that Ann had entered a more perilous stage of her pregnancy. Ann's normally radiant, cheerful eyes were subdued; her smile was weak and her voice was rather emotionless.

Her expression brightened considerably when Bob walked in. He went directly to the bed and kissed his wife. Jessie saw tears in Ann's eyes and felt the deep, abiding love between her brother and his wife. Quietly, she got up and left the room.

Going downstairs to the kitchen, Jessie heated some more of the soup and sat down at the table with a small bowl. Her own appetite was barely an acknowledgment that she'd eaten nothing since breakfast with Hank.

She sighed softly, recalling her plans to have a candid discussion with first her brother and then with Hank. Bob's energies were concentrated on Ann; he couldn't possibly be in a mood to hear a long tale of trouble and woe. As for Hank, Jessie still felt it imperative to talk to Bob first.

Actually, mulling it all over, she would have little time for Hank or anything else until the baby came. What she had told Dr. Haley was the gospel: she wouldn't leave Ann's side for a minute, not unless Bob was with her. Mavis was a good housekeeper, but she had her own life. The Shroeders should and would depend on one another for Ann's safety.

Jessie was rinsing her dishes when Bob carried Ann's tray into the kitchen. "How is she doing?" Jessie asked.

Bob set the tray on the counter. "All right, I think. She ate most of her dinner."

"Did you talk to Dr. Haley?"

"Yes." Bob rubbed the back of his neck in a weary gesture. "He's considering hospitalization, but not without some reluctance."

"That's what he told me, too. He said he wanted to discuss it with you. What's your opinion?"

"I talked to Ann about it. She's willing to do whatever Ralph thinks best, of course, but she would like to stay at home as long as possible."

"That's understandable," Jessie quietly agreed. "Bob, does Thorp's small hospital have the facilities Ann might need in an emergency?"

Bob shook his head. "It's only equipped for normal childbirth. We've been planning all along to take Ann to Cheyenne for the final two weeks of her term."

"Then hospitalization would mean going to Cheyenne right away?"

"That's another gray area. I don't know, Jessie. Ann's been doing so well. Ralph said she could have some bad days, and I guess we're all hoping that's all today was. He's going to start dropping by every morning to check on her."

"He's very conscientious."

"He's more than a good doctor, Ralph's a friend. He suggested a nurse, but in talking about it, he really only wants someone with Ann at all times. Jessie, I'm in the middle of a complex lawsuit. It's not impossible to put everything on hold for a few months, but it would be difficult."

"That's not necessary. Nor is hiring someone to stay with Ann. I'm happy to do it, Bob." She felt her brother's probing gaze. Drying her hands on a paper towel, Jessie met it. "I mean that. Ann will never be left alone again."

"What about Hank?"

There was so much behind that question, tension, disapproval, curiosity. "Hank understands," Jessie said with a finality that didn't invite debate. She wasn't going to get into another argument with Bob, not about Hank, not even about Allen. When the time was right, she would explain everything.

Right now, they were all focused on Ann and the baby, which was only sensible. A serious situation demanded serious measures, and Jessie was very willing to put her own problems and plans aside for the time being. Hank would not desert her just because she was going to be busy with Ann, and besides, Bob would be home most evenings. Hank's own work took up most of his days, and they could see each other in the evenings.

Bob finally nodded. "I hope you know how much I appreciate your being here. Like I said, it's not impossible to change my schedule, and I would do it before risking Ann and the baby. But there is another... consideration."

Jessie noted the strangely embarrassed look on her brother's face. For a man who rarely showed anyone other than his wife his personal feelings, embarrassment was like a red flag, alerting Jessie, stirring her curiosity.

Bob cleared his throat. "Ann and I... well, we've had a lot of medical bills to pay. Our insurance covers only a fraction of the actual costs, you see, and—"

"You're short of money," Jessie interjected softly. That possibility had never occurred to her. Bob, like herself, had inherited a nice sum of cash at their parents' deaths. Hers had gone to Allen, and now she realized that Bob's had gone to doctors and hospitals. No wonder he had some hesitancy about putting his legal practice "on hold" to spend his time with Ann.

Jessie sighed sadly. She could offer what she had, the money in that California bank that the elder Vaughns had pressed on her. But she knew Bob wasn't hinting for money. An offer would no doubt appall him. All he was doing was making his position clearer than it had been, giving her another reason why her presence was so appreciated.

"It's all right, Bob. Please don't even consider hiring a nurse." Jessie's smile contained all the love she felt for this normally stern, overly proud man. "We'll get Ann and the baby through this, I promise."

Hank called very early the next morning. "I'm taking a charter out, Jessie, and probably won't be back until late."

"I guess dinner's off in that case," she murmured.

"I'm sorry. I wanted tonight together."

"It's okay, Hank. Bob might be late, too."

"I could call when I get home. If it's not too late, you could come over."

There was a ring of adolescence in the conversation, as though they were plotting something they had no right to do behind someone's back. It seemed so inane that Hank couldn't just come to the house.

But Jessie didn't want to make waves at the present. Everything else had come to a standstill because of Ann's dire situation, and insisting that Hank and Bob face each other right now would only cause distress that none of them needed.

"Maybe tomorrow night," she sighed with resignation.

"Tomorrow night for certain," Hank replied firmly. "I miss you, Jessie."

"I miss you, too." It was true. Missing Hank was a dull throb in her body. Concentrating on Ann was at the forefront of her thoughts, but Hank's image was always there, behind everything else she did and said. He wasn't far away, only a few miles, but he wasn't close enough to touch, and that's what she needed, physical contact and the unique emotional rapport she felt with him.

"What are you doing right now?" Hank asked softly.

"Getting dressed."

"You're alone in your room?"

"Yes, why?"

"I just got out of the shower."

"You're naked?" she whispered, suddenly very hot and achy. After the other night in Hank's camper, just the thought of him naked packed a sexual wallop.

"I wish you were here," Hank said huskily.

Jessie tried to laugh. "I wish I were, too."

"Tomorrow night, Jessie."

"Definitely."

All day, Jessie felt as if circumstances and everyone involved were building to some kind of crescendo. She couldn't lay her finger on the root of the feeling. The letter from Allen was part of it, Ann's continuing lethargy was part of it, Bob's tension, Hank's tension, her own, were all part of it. It was an intuitive feeling, sort of like the disquietude one experienced just before an electrical storm hit.

While she tended to Ann's needs and talked to her in only the most soothing tones, Jessie couldn't shake the ominous sensation. True, all of her own plans were indefinitely delayed, and maybe she couldn't help wishing that things were different. It seemed to her that her life had taken an abrupt upswing a few days ago and now hung in a precarious limbo. Maybe that was it. Maybe she was on edge because a decision once made was difficult to stifle.

Bob was late getting home again and arrived with apologies and questions about Ann. "She slept a good portion of the day," Jessie told him, adding with a smile, "I know she's anxious to see you."

After Bob had gone upstairs, Jessie sighed and curled up on the sofa. The next three months could be very long. If she had told everyone the truth about her marriage when she first came home, Bob would understand why any thoughts of reconciliation with Allen were ludicrous. That's what was really standing in the way of the possibility of friendship between Hank and Bob, her brother's feeling that Hank was once again interfering in Jessie's life.

Someday, she hoped with a dejected sigh, her family and Hank would be friends. She couldn't hurry the process, no one could at this point. Her uneasiness and that intuitive dread bothering her weren't going to go away, either. Not until everyone understood one another.

Dear God, would that ever really happen?

Twelve

At nearly eleven the next day, Ann cried out in pain. Jessie was sitting right there beside her bed. They had been talking about the college each of them had attended, exchanging anecdotes, discussing professors, attitudes, favorite classes. It was only girl talk about nothing very important, but it was something Jessie realized she hadn't been a part of for years. Her "friends" in California had been chosen by Allen. She had nothing there, not even a friend of her own.

They were laughing at a remark Ann had made, and then she cried out. Jessie froze for a moment, but her wits returned very quickly. "What is it, Ann?"

The spasm had passed, but Ann's eyes were spilling tears and she was holding the lower half of her rounded abdomen. "Oh, Jessie," she whispered. "It's the baby. I don't think this is another false alarm. Please call Dr. Haley."

Jessie knew the trembling of her hands on the telephone was perfectly obvious, but she couldn't seem to remain altogether steady. Ann was in labor and it was too soon!

She relayed a brief, urgent message to Dr. Haley, then called Bob, who was, thank God, in town today. "Dr. Haley is on his way, Bob."

"I'll be home in five minutes."

Ann's eyes were frightened and teary. "I'm going to lose the baby," she said on a sob. "Oh, Jessie, I can't bear it. I've done everything right, everything the doctor said to do."

Wanting to weep herself, Jessie sat on the bed and took her sister-in-law's small hand. "Be brave, Annie. Many babies come early. Be very strong and very brave."

She was still holding Ann's hand, still willing her and her baby to get through this safely, when Bob came running in. Dr. Haley was no more than thirty seconds behind him. "I need to examine her," the doctor stated immediately.

Bob stayed with his wife, but Jessie stepped out to the hall. Leaning against the wall, she bit her lip until it hurt to keep from crying. She could hear Dr. Haley's questions and Ann's answers, and it seemed to take an eternity before anything was decided.

"This could be false labor again," the doctor finally announced. "But it appears more serious this time and I don't think we should take the chance. I'll call the hospital and make arrangements for Ann's admission."

"Here, in Thorp?" Bob didn't sound very pleased. It came to Jessie that he might be upset because the doctor hadn't insisted on Ann's hospitalization two days ago.

"Bob, it's a long ride to Cheyenne," the doctor said gently.

"I know it is!" Jessie peered around the door to see her brother's agitation, which was apparent in every line of his body. His stress was genuine, affecting Jessie in a wave of sisterly love. Bob and Ann were so dear to her, her family, and their problems were, indeed, hers, too. How wrong she had been to hide her own distress, how very wrong.

It wasn't a long ride in a helicopter! Why that thought suddenly came to Jessie she would never know, but she knew she had to get it across to Bob. She stepped through the door. "Bob, Ann could be flown to Cheyenne."

"Flown?" Bob stopped to consider the idea, and Jessie knew that money and time and worry for his wife and child were all going through his mind.

"Hank's helicopter," Jessie said quietly, planting the seed a little deeper.

Dr. Haley's left eyebrow shot up. "Hank Farrell's helicopter! That's a darned good idea, Jessie. Bob, maybe I should have hospitalized Ann a few days ago, but I honestly believed she was all right."

"I know that, Ralph," Bob said with a thoughtful frown. He looked at Jessie. "Do you think Hank would consider forgetting the past and flying us to Cheyenne?"

"Of course, he would." Jessie wasn't kidding either herself or her brother. After Hank's comments about him and Bob getting to know each other better, she truly believed he would welcome the opportunity to put them on a sounder footing. Besides, what did old grudges matter when Ann and her baby were in possible danger? "Shall I call him?"

Bob lifted his chin and squared his shoulders. "Thanks, but I'll call him myself." He walked out of the room.

Jessie went over to Ann. "I'll pack a suitcase for you."

"Thank you, Jessie," Ann whispered.

As timing went, things could have been much worse. Busily filling a small suitcase with the things Ann would need, Jessie thought about how dire this emergency could have been if it had occurred only yesterday. Hank had been out on a charter and Bob had been in Sheridan. They were all very fortunate that it had happened today.

Bob returned. "Hank's waiting on the phone. He wants to talk to you," he told his sister.

"Will he do it?"

"Yes. He'll have the copter ready by the time we get to his place."

Jessie breathed a sigh of relief, then hurried out of the room to talk to Hank in private. Bob had gone downstairs for the call, she knew, so she raced down to the living room.

The phone was off the hook and she hastily picked it up. "Hank?"

"Hi. Bob's call surprised the heck out of me. What's your opinion of Ann's condition?"

"I think she's in labor, Hank. The doctor isn't positive, however, so I guess we'll just have to wait and see. She does need to go to the hospital, though."

"Bob said that Dr. Haley is coming along."

"I'm sure he is."

"Jessie, there won't be room in the helicopter for you."

"I know."

"I'll call you from Cheyenne."

"Please do. I'll be on pins and needles until I hear something."

"Goodbye, honey. I'll see you tonight."

"I'll be waiting."

Bob came down the stairs with his wife in his arms. Dr. Haley was right behind him, carrying Ann's suitcase and his own medical bag. Mavis was standing in the hall, as worried looking as the rest of them. "Lord have mercy," she whispered.

"Ann will be fine," Jessie said in a sharp undertone, refusing to get weepy and emotional where her sister-in-law might get a glimpse of it.

The small entourage filed through the house and out the front door, with Jessie and Mavis trailing behind. Bob tucked his wife into the back seat of his car, then he and Dr. Haley got into the front. "I'll phone from Cheyenne," Bob called out as he closed the car door and started the engine.

Jessie nodded. She and Mavis stood on the porch and waved as the car backed out of the driveway and sped off. Then she saw Mavis wipe her eyes and softened toward the older woman. "We can't think the worst," she said on a sigh, and led Mavis back into the house.

"This is going to be a long afternoon," Mavis said gloomily.

"Yes, it is," Jessie agreed. "Mavis, if you have something you'd like to do, feel free to leave. There's not much point to your hanging around here all afternoon."

"Well, I've been meaning to get my dress altered." Mavis had shown off the pretty dress she had bought in Cheyenne, and had announced that it needed a few alterations to fit perfectly.

"Go and take care of it. There's no reason for you to cook dinner tonight, and anything else you planned to do in the house today can wait."

"You're sure you don't mind?"

"I'm very sure."

Mavis practically ran to get her purse, but she did stop on the way out. "Jessie, I'll be calling later to find out how Ann is doing."

"All right."

With the closing of the door behind Mavis, Jessie admitted that she was glad to be alone. That strange, edgy feeling she had endured yesterday now felt like a premonition. Poor Ann, she thought. Poor Bob. Oh, please, please let their baby be all right.

Jessie spent the ensuing hours in critical self-analysis. The mess she had made of her life seemed to be less convoluted. Her memories as Mrs. Allen Vaughn would always be painful, no matter how much time passed, but Hank's influence was stronger than the past. She really, truly loved that man, and when this was over—*happily* over, she continued to pray—she was going to tell Hank everything, but especially how she felt about him.

Could she even doubt that he loved her, too? Hadn't he practically announced his feelings the night he'd picked her up and brought her to his place? Some part of Hank Farrell had never stopped loving Jessie Shroeder, and she could say the exact same thing about herself. She loved Hank and it was time to face it.

Jessie's insides suddenly coiled. It wasn't that simple, no matter how much she wished it were. How was Hank going to take her story? What would he think of a woman who had put up with what she had for eight years?

Kelsy had told her to trust people's intelligence. *Normal people are appalled at such behavior, Jessie. You must stop thinking that anyone who learns about your marriage is going to blame you.*

It was the one point that Jessie kept butting her head against. Allen's violence wasn't her fault. Intellectually, she believed that. But the shame went so deep, penetrating every private sector of herself. How did she purge shame from her system? How did she look Hank—and Bob—in the eye and confess that she had allowed such punishment to go on for so long?

When the telephone finally rang, Jessie was well within reach and picked it up on its first ring. "Hello, honey."

"Oh, Hank. I'm so glad you called. What's going on?"

"Bob said to tell you that Ann is doing okay. She's in the maternity ward with all kinds of monitors and specialists watching her. They're still not certain that she *is* in labor, but it's a distinct possibility."

Jessie's heart sank. "Has anyone made a prognosis yet? Is the baby all right?"

"So far, so good, Jessie. That's really all I know. I'm starting back to Thorp in a few minutes. Bob is staying in Cheyenne, naturally."

"Yes, of course."

"By the way, we got along pretty well. He's a good guy, Jessie. I don't think I've ever seen any man more concerned with his wife."

"Bob and Ann love each other very much."

"That's completely obvious. Anyway, I'm anxious to see you. Are you holding up? I hated going off and leaving you behind."

"It couldn't be helped, Hank. I'm anxious to see you, too." Jessie hesitated, then added, "There's something I have to tell you. I had thought it best to tell Bob first, but I know now that you're the one I need to talk to before anyone else."

"Is it about your marriage, Jessie?"

"Yes," she whispered, gripping the phone too hard, battling that knotting sensation in her stomach again.

"You can tell me anything, honey. Don't sound so scared."

"Be very brave and very strong," she had told Ann. It was good advice for herself, too. "Fly carefully, but quickly," she said, trying very hard to inject a little humor into her voice.

"See you in two hours."

Putting the phone down, Jessie glanced around the silent room. Two hours to kill until Hank arrived. She had to do something besides worry.

Forcing herself to move, Jessie went to the kitchen and opened a cookbook.

A double batch of spicy oatmeal cookies cooling on aluminum foil on the counter was sending a sweet, rich aroma throughout the house. Jessie finished eating her third cookie and checked the time. Hank should be coming along any minute now.

She'd had noticeable difficulty breathing normally for the past two hours. Regardless of determination and common sense, baring her soul to Hank was going to be the hardest thing she had ever done.

In her upstairs bathroom, Jessie brushed her hair and dabbed on a light layer of lipstick. Bob had called, but with very little more information than Hank had related. "Ann is being carefully monitored. So far, Jessie, thank God, both she and the baby are all right."

Jessie clung to that thought as she prepared for Hank's arrival. Her heart insisted on thudding, and she was positive that she was paler than usual. But most of the day had been traumatic, and it was far from over yet.

She *would* get through it, Jessie swore. She planned to hold nothing back with Hank, not her own doubts and fears, not any of Allen's instability. Hank could make up his own mind about her role in the nightmare.

But, of course, that was the core of her dread, how Hank would feel about it all.

The front doorbell chimed and Jessie paused only long enough for a final look at herself in the mirror before hurrying down to the first floor. Her pulse was beating abnormally fast when she reached for the doorknob and she paused again, this time for a deep breath.

She opened the door, then went completely still. It wasn't Hank standing there, it was Allen.

"Hello, Jessie."

His blond good looks offended her, his obsequious smile frightened her. She backed up a step, then realized that she had given him room to come in. Her head was spinning, threatening blackness. With a fearful cry, she attempted to push the door closed.

Laughing softly, Allen took control of it and held it open. "Say hello, Jessie."

The emptiness of the house mocked her, and she could barely breathe. "What—what are you doing here?" she finally managed to choke out.

"I told you in my letter that I was coming to see you."

Jessie's stomach churned with nausea. Pretending that letter didn't exist had been foolhardy. Her head felt ready to burst with increased blood pressure. She was alone here, and all of the fear she had lived with for eight years was returning and turning her limbs to jelly.

But that was what Allen wanted. She could see the sly, triumphant look in his eyes. This was what made him feel powerful, having her cowering and on the verge of collapse.

Jessie's voice cracked from strain. "You're not welcome here." She saw the light of battle enter his eyes. "Leave or I'll call the sheriff," she rasped.

With one hand, Allen maintained his hold on the door, while he held the other one up in a placating gesture that Jessie saw as utterly hollow, completely false. "What am I doing wrong? A man talking to his wife is hardly a crime, Jessie."

"I'm not your wife."

His eyes narrowed. "You'll always be my wife. Now, let me come in. You're being ridiculous, as usual." He didn't wait for agreement, he merely pushed the door open wider and stepped into the foyer.

Jessie backed up again when he closed the door behind him and then leaned against it, almost nonchalantly. She saw him listening, measuring the house for sounds. "You're home alone, aren't you?" he said in a lethally quiet voice.

"Ann is upstairs," she hastily lied. "And Bob will be home any minute."

His eyes bored into hers. "You're lying, Jessie. No one's here but you. What exquisite timing." He smiled, only there wasn't a drop of humor or warmth in the expression, and Jessie's heart nearly stopped beating. When he pushed away from the door, she retreated again and a forward step of his resulted in another backward step of hers. "You should be glad to see me," he said in that deadly tone of voice Jessie had learned to dread.

"We're divorced," she whispered, unable to speak with courage when she had none. Every contour of Allen's body was a threat. He had proven again and again how capable he was of violence.

Disdainfully, he snapped his fingers. "That's what I think of that piece of paper."

He kept coming and Jessie kept retreating. Her eyes were wide and frightened and glued to Allen's face. He had the upper hand and he knew it, and there was a twisted pleasure intermingled with the cold cruelty in his eyes. This was what he liked, Jessie knew, her backing up, him advancing. For years and years, she had walked on eggs to avoid this very scenario. He would corner her somewhere and then talk to her as though she were a naughty child. His rage would fester within a quiet voice and vile accusations, and then, when he was angry enough, he would slap her. If she took it meekly, that sometimes was the end of it, but if she showed the slightest resistance, the slaps would go on. And on.

She must get him talking. It was the only way. Get him involved in a long lecture on her supposed transgressions. Her mind raced. Hank should be arriving, unless something unforeseen had delayed him. Hank. Just the thought of him helped.

"I didn't get your letter," she breathlessly lied. Allen stopped, a moment of doubt crossing his face.

"Bob didn't get my letter? I put yours in with his."

"No... no, he didn't. When did you mail it?"

"Over a week ago. It should have beat me here by several days." Allen's eyes narrowed on her. "Are you lying again?"

"No! That's why I was so surprised to see you." She saw his expression change, take on a speculative note.

"You *were* surprised. Maybe you're telling the truth for once."

He had always accused her of lying, which, sadly, was more truth than fiction. But he had never allowed her to be herself. At the very beginning of their marriage, before she had known how dangerous honesty was, her natural candor had caused some terrifying scenes. She had resorted to lies for the sake of self-preservation.

"I—I just baked some cookies," she said breathlessly. "Maybe you would like a cup of coffee."

"No coffee," he snapped. "Talk, Jessie, that's what I want. Conversation."

Her knees were wobbling and she used the back of a chair for support. "Did you drive?"

"My car's out front."

She saw him looking around and listening again. "Where's Ann? And that housekeeper of hers?"

"Ann's not well," Jessie mumbled. His eyes rose to the ceiling.

"Is she really upstairs?"

Should she lie again? He might go upstairs and check, and if he did...? "She's in the hospital," Jessie admitted, her numb lips making speech difficult.

"Another lie." Allen sighed dramatically. "That's all that ever comes out of your mouth, lies. Jessie, what am I going to do with you?"

"What did you want to talk about?" she interjected quickly.

His eyes darkened. "Us. You're coming back to California with me."

My God. Jessie's insides wound into a tighter ball. She licked her dry lips. "I...can't leave. I promised Bob I would stay with Ann for the summer."

"If she's in the hospital, what good are you doing her?"

Panic was nearly destroying Jessie's thin hold on composure. She wanted to run, but Allen was blocking the path to the door. "She won't be there very long, and when she comes home, I have to be here."

"What a good little sister-in-law," Allen sneered. "Go pack your things. You'd be as much of a detriment to her as you were to me."

Jessie's chin was quivering. "I *was* a detriment to you, so why do you want me back?"

His mouth twisted. "Because you belong to me, that's why!"

"I belong to no one! People don't belong to other people!" She saw the rage on his face and cringed from it, but she couldn't stop this small spurt of rebellion. "Allen, please go away. Just leave me alone. We're divorced. You have no right to be here."

He advanced again, cold fury on his face. "Don't tell me about my rights. Who did you pick up that garbage from, anyway, that counselor you've been seeing in L.A.?"

Jessie moved around the chair, putting it between them. "What about your counselor? You've been seeing someone, too. What kind of advice have you been getting? It wasn't this, Allen. No professional told you it was all right to come here and harass me."

"I'm not harassing you! I'm here to take you home. Even you should be able to see the difference." He stopped at the edge of the chair. "Go and pack, Jessie. I'm warning you, my patience is coming to an end."

Jessie began to hope. Allen had never "warned" her before. Before the divorce, he wouldn't have tolerated even a fraction of the resistance she'd just shown him. She drew in a long, shaky breath. "Allen—"

"Go and pack, Jessie. *Now!*"

She honestly didn't see the blow coming. His arm moved so quickly, reaching across the chair, that she saw nothing except a blur. But she felt the stinging slap that caught her cheek and nose and knocked her backward two reeling steps. Dazed, her hand went to her nose, and she looked at the blood on her fingers.

Tears of frustration and from that old, debilitating sense of helplessness began to drip down her cheeks. "You're insane," she whispered.

It was the wrong thing to have said, she instantly realized. Allen's rage was completely out of control now and he darted around the chair and grabbed her by the arm. His wrath spewed forth in vicious curses and his hand raised to deliver another slap.

Jessie's head rocked from its force. She heard herself weeping, begging.

Hank gave the car with the California license plates parked at the curb a brief glance, then proceeded up the Shroeders' front walk at an eager pace. All during the flight from Cheyenne, he had anticipated this moment. It was what he had been waiting for since the night Jessie had jumped out of his pickup and tried to run away rather than talk about what was bothering her.

There was too much between them to continue pretending otherwise. If he'd had an ounce of sense at Jessie's return to Thorp, he'd have known that just seeing her would bring everything back.

The thing was, "everything" was only a trickle of what he felt for Jessie now. Maybe it was because they were older, maybe because they had both grown up in the past eight years. But just thinking of Jessie elicited images of children and growing old together. Her declaration about having something to tell him warmed a soul that Hank now knew had been shriveling. How much real satisfaction did a man get out of working himself into exhaustion and watching his net worth increase?

He wanted a family. He wanted a son, a daughter, maybe more than one of each, whatever the good Lord sent to him and Jessie. He wanted his house to ring with life and laughter, with kids and love, lots and lots of love.

Hank put a foot on the first step of the Shroeders' front porch. He had things to tell Jessie, too. Bob Shroeder had impressed the heck out of him, and he'd felt the man's respect. Something important had happened during that flight to Cheyenne. He and Bob had seen each other differently than they ever had, and Hank couldn't imagine a reason for either of them to hold back friendship any longer.

With a grin just slightly short of silly, Hank took the rest of the stairs in a single leap. He felt as though he'd lost a hundred pounds somewhere that afternoon. Everything seemed to be working out and he was itching to see Jessie, to hold her, to tell her how much he loved her.

At the door, he stopped to ring the bell. And then, just as his hand reached the button, he heard voices, a man's, speaking harshly, a woman's, strangely strangled.

From inside? Hesitating, Hank tensed and listened. It took a moment to register the level of dark emotions he was hearing, another second to recognize the crying woman as Jessie. His heart went wild and he grabbed the doorknob.

It wouldn't turn; the door was locked.

The sounds from within the house were becoming more distinct. Each of his own increasingly frantic heartbeats brought a clearer picture of what was going on. Jessie was in danger. A man was in there with her.

There was no decision to make. Stepping back from the door, Hank made a powerful lunge against it. It swung open with the first assault. He crossed the threshold into the foyer on a dead run, then stopped at the rounded archway to the living room.

The scene shocked his senses. He'd only seen Allen Vaughn one time in his life, but the man holding Jessie's arm with his left hand and standing with his right hand raised, poised for a blow, instantly connected in Hank's mind with the California license plate.

No one moved. It seemed, for a long, deathly still moment, that no one even breathed. Jessie's nose was bleeding. Her face was wet with tears and blood. Allen was staring at Hank, as though the devil himself had suddenly walked into the room. Hank's gaze darted back and forth between the cowering, pale woman and the man standing over her.

And then, a red haze of blind rage infiltrated Hank's shock. He had never felt murder in his veins before, but he suddenly wanted to destroy Allen Vaughn. He wanted to tear him apart with his bare hands, to give him double, triple, of what he had just given a small, defenseless woman.

Within his first two purposeful steps, Hank knew exactly what it was that Jessie had been hiding. The sudden, stunning knowledge was like taking a hard blow to the stomach. His mouth shaped curses. His eyes narrowed to furious slits. He saw Allen let go of Jessie's arm and begin to back up, causing Hank to change directions.

He stalked the man, going slowly, enjoying the fear on his weak, sallow face. "You son of a bitch," Hank said, his voice low and tense. His hands clenched into fists, every muscle in his body tautened and prepared for the vengeance he planned to take.

"Hank..."

It was a low moan from Jessie, and Hank looked to see her clinging to a chair, as though her legs weren't strong enough to hold her up. He looked back at Allen. The man was sidling around the room, hoping to reach the door before Hank reached him. Vaughn's fear was so palpable, Hank could smell it.

Jessie... Allen... which one? This time there *was* a decision to make. Bloodying Vaughn's face was only just... but Jessie was already bleeding.

And weeping, softly now, as though she didn't even have the strength needed to cry. Hank felt like crying, too. His Jessie, bleeding because of this man.

Allen hadn't ignored the opportunity provided by Hank's indecision. Inch by inch, he had almost gained the archway. Hank turned his back on him and went to Jessie, tenderly gathering her up into his arms. She clung to him and he knew that he'd done the right thing, coming to her. She'd had just about all of the violence she could take.

"*Vaughn!*" Hank's voice lashed the air and the man stopped at the archway. "I want you to listen to this real good. Get out of Thorp. Get out of Wyoming. If I ever even hear of you anywhere within a hundred miles of Jessie again, I'll find you. Do you understand?"

The man nodded with some sullenness, and Hank repeated, in a voice heavily laden with barely controlled rage and utter contempt, "*Do you understand?*"

"I'm going. I understand."

"Don't ever doubt that I mean it." Hank was actually trembling. He knew that it would take only one hint of smugness or one tiny misstep from that foul piece of humanity in the doorway, and he wouldn't be able to stop himself from beating him into the ground.

Jessie was trembling, too, and Hank knew that it was her small body clinging to his that was saving Vaughn from what was only justice. She felt as fragile as a snowflake in his arms.

And that wretched piece of garbage had hit her!

Over her head, Hank watched Vaughn disappear through the archway, then listened to the man's hasty footsteps through the foyer.

He closed his eyes, attempting to stop the tears he felt gathering. But they seeped down his cheeks and onto Jessie's dark hair. A spasm of grief started in his belly and worked its way up to his throat, choking him, making his comforting words garbled, nearly unintelligible. "He's gone... you're safe... he'll never hurt you again... never... never..."

Thirteen

It was over. For the first time, Jessie felt completely segregated from Allen. It was strange, that feeling, because legally and in almost every other way, she'd been free of him for some time. Unhappily, however, and so very much against Jessie's heartfelt prayers, there had been something of him remaining until now, a tightening of muscle and marrow at his name, an unconscious flinching at his memory.

Hank had bathed the blood from her face and put cold packs on her bruises. He had wanted her to lie down, but she'd had something to take care of first. "Would you drive me to the sheriff's office?" she had asked.

The forced entry and assault-and-battery charges she filed against Allen had been for Hank. Whatever else happened in the future, Jessie didn't want Hank getting into trouble, and if Allen ever dared show his face in the area again, Hank *would* get into trouble. A good beating might be just what Allen deserved, but she didn't want Hank administering it and then facing charges himself.

Jessie also planned to write to Allen's parents and let them know that if Allen was seen in Wyoming again, he would be put under arrest. She *would* go to court and testify against him, and she *would* do anything and everything in her power to put him behind bars. With two threats hanging over his head, the state of Wyoming *and* Hank Farrell, he just might figure out this was no place for him to be hanging around.

There were other plans in Jessie's mind, too. For one thing, she was going to use that money the Vaughns had insisted on giving her at the time of the divorce. It was little enough for eight years of abuse and, really, only repayment of the inheritance Allen had forced her to hand over. She would open her dress shop. As for any hope of a future with Hank, they still had some talking to do.

They were sitting on the living room sofa with one lamp burning. The room was shadowed and quiet. Hank was holding her hand. To him, there was a foreignness about being in this house. Its high ceilings and old-fashioned charm were akin to his memories of Jessie's parents, formal and dignified. He'd never been welcome here before, and he knew that familiarity with the place would take some time.

But those thoughts were minor, insignificant right now. He felt such a oneness with Jessie. Secrets had vanished and her past heartaches were his to console. "You couldn't talk about it, could you?" Hank said softly.

Jessie studied the way his big hand was curled around hers, a posture that concealed her eyes. She had looked at Hank many times in the past hour, but right now, with this subject naked and pitiful before them, she just couldn't do it. "I was ashamed."

"Why, Jessie? You were the victim. Why would *you* feel shame?"

"I know it's hard to understand. Before I came home, I was seeing a counselor, Hank. Her name is Kelsy Worth, and she works with..." Jessie hesitated at the term. "...battered women," she finished in a near whisper.

Hank felt all of the repugnance at the term that Jessie had known he would. "Battered women" was a particularly abhorrent phrase. Like "abused children." Like "cruelty to animals." What the hell was wrong with the human race that its members could attack those weaker than themselves? How did people like Allen Vaughn face themselves in a mirror?

It made Hank's skin crawl every time he allowed the reality of what he knew now to surface: Jessie had been slapped and knocked around on a regular basis. Today's abuse was what she had lived with for eight years. No wonder she had come home thin and looking like she hadn't a friend in the world. No wonder her eyes hadn't shone and she had recoiled from an innocent touch.

But, my Lord, should the abused, the victims, feel shame over it? Why would she take any of the blame for her own maltreatment? That attitude made no sense to Hank.

"You're a strong, capable man, Hank," Jessie went on. "You've never been afraid of anyone or anything. Women..." She hesitated again. Maybe all women didn't feel their lack of physical strength as keenly as she did. Most women had little reason to compare their lesser strength with a man's. How often she had wished for the brawn to stand up to Allen! "You don't know what it's like to be the weaker sex," she said quietly.

"No, I know I don't. But there's more to it than physical strength, Jessie. Men like Allen have a loose screw. Thank God there aren't many of them around."

Jessie raised her head and met Hank's kindly blue eyes. "That's what I used to believe, too. But Kelsy told me that there are a lot more women in the position I was in than the thinking public suspects." Kelsy had also said that the very reason the mistreatment wasn't better publicized was because many wives and girlfriends did exactly what Jessie had done: accepted the blame. The men doing the battering were masters at manipulation, knowing when to show remorse, knowing how to beg and plead for forgiveness, making empty promises over and over again.

If she would have had the opportunity to talk to some-one like Kelsy in the first year of her marriage, for that matter, in the first two weeks of her marriage, Jessie felt that her whole life might have been different.

But then, she thought with a wistful look at Hank, she might not be here with him now. Life was such a circuitous road, and how could she second-guess hers when it had ul-timately brought her back to Hank?

Her emotions were very raw and tender, Jessie realized when her eyes misted over. Hank brushed a lock of her hair back from her face. "Did you ever really love him, Jes-sie?"

She would never, ever be anything but honest with Hank again, but she wished she could evade that question. She couldn't, though. He had the right to know everything she had ever thought and felt. "I thought I did," she whis-pered sadly, and saw the hurt she had expected in his eyes. "It was different than what I felt for you."

"You were afraid of me."

A shiver prickled Jessie's skin. It seemed almost insane to admit she'd been afraid of Hank, when the man she had chosen had treated her so vilely. But she could qualify that old fear. "Not you personally, Hank. Your reputation. How my parents and most of the town perceived you."

Hank laid his head back on the sofa and released a dis-satisfied sigh. "I was totally self-centered, except where you were concerned. I would have done anything for you, Jes-sie."

"No, Hank, you wouldn't have," she denied softly. When he looked at her queerly, she added, "You weren't able to change yourself for me any more than I was able to change myself for you. We both thought we were trying very hard, didn't we? Isn't that how you remember it, that you really worked at winning over the town?"

He felt the blood draining his face. "You know I didn't."

She nodded slowly. "And I didn't fight for you, either. We thought we were in love, and neither one of us did any more than talk about it."

He swallowed the sudden lump in his throat, then reached out and drew her to him. "I could have taken a stand with my parents," Jessie whispered into his shirt. "I was old enough to get married and I didn't have to let Mother and Father or anyone else influence my judgment."

Hank felt like the wind had just been knocked out of him. So many wasted years. So much unnecessary unhappiness. And he'd blamed Jessie for eight long years, when he was every bit as responsible for the past as she was. More, probably. In retrospect, he saw that it would have taken very little effort to show the Shroeders that there was more to him than they'd believed. "You're right. I could have changed," he said with some bitterness. "I did after you left."

"Oh, Hank," she whispered, and felt his arms tighten around her.

He kissed the top of her head. "I love you, Jessie. I've loved you since you were fourteen years old."

Jessie lifted her head and looked into his eyes. "I love you, Hank. There are times now when I think that I've loved you all of my life."

"I'll never hurt you."

"I know."

There were tears in his eyes. "Not tonight, not now—I honestly don't think I could bear hearing the details of what you lived through with that jackass right now—but some-day, Jessie, when my nerves are steadier and you're calmer, then I want the whole story."

"Yes," she agreed huskily, gratefully. If Hank had wanted to discuss the specifics of her marriage tonight, she was ready for it, but deep down, she was greatly relieved that he didn't.

He smoothed her hair back. "I don't want you feeling shame," he said in a voice ragged with emotion. "You don't deserve that, Jessie. You were always so sweet, so—"

"Malleable? Manageable? Impressionable? I got those words from Kelsy, Hank. I remember myself as obedient, overly conscientious about others' opinions. It's very sad that my parents never got to know you, and it's equally sad that you never really knew them. They were good people. Their mistakes were with the best of intentions."

Hank sighed regretfully. "I found that out about Bob today. He's a straitlaced son-of-a-gun, but—" The ringing of the telephone interrupted. "Maybe that's Bob now."

Jessie drew a hopeful breath and slipped out of Hank's arms. She hadn't forgotten Ann in everything else that had taken place and she hurried to the phone. "Hello?"

"Jessie...we have a daughter." Bob was crying, Jessie was sure of it. His voice was as rusty as old nails, thick with emotion. "They took her by cesarean section. She's the tiniest, most beautiful little thing you've ever seen. She's in the hospital's special preemie unit, but she's healthy, Jessie, healthy! Ann's still waking up, but she's fine, too."

"Oh, Bob, I'm so happy for you." Jessie sent Hank a thumbs-up gesture and a teary smile. Elated, he got to his feet and went to stand beside her while she talked to her brother.

Bob was full of data about the operation and the birth of his daughter, which spilled out of him with an enthusiasm that made Jessie want to laugh for the pure joy of it. She would tell Bob everything about the past and today, too, but not now. Not when he was so wonderfully, blissfully happy.

He finally ran down, and Jessie could tell that he was anxious to get back to his wife. "Give Ann my love," she told him.

"I will. Bye, Jessie."

"Goodbye, Bob."

She was about to put the phone down when she heard, "Jessie!"

"Yes?"

"There's something I want to say. It's about Hank."

Jessie reached out and placed her hand on Hank's chest. His eyes warmed, and he took her hand and brought it to his lips. She had purplish bruises on the left side of her face, and looking at them gave him a sensation that felt like acid eating at his vitals. He could easily squash Allen Vaughn like the insect he was, and he would have already done so if Jessie hadn't been reeling and needing comfort a lot more than revenge. But if the man ever dared to come near her again, there wouldn't be enough left of him *to* arrest and slap in jail.

That was his own private vow, the one that kept Hank from throwing something or from getting in his car and going out looking for Vaughn.

Jessie was holding the telephone to her right ear, and Hank bent forward and pressed a tender kiss to her left. She loved him, just as he loved her, and the trauma of the past eight years was disappearing in the wonder of knowing that they would be together from here on in.

"What about Hank?" Jessie said into the phone with some breathlessness, a result of Hank's nearness, his touch, so unlike anyone else's, gentleness with a vibrant core of sensuality. She heard Bob clearing his throat.

"Well . . . I guess it's nothing more than that I never gave Hank a chance. None of us did. He was great today, Jessie. I feel a little foolish about a grudge that maybe never did have any real foundation."

Jessie smiled. "Oh, it had foundation, Bob. But we've all changed. For the better, I'm willing to bet."

"Anyway, Jessie, I know you like him and—"

"No, you're wrong, Bob. I don't just like Hank, I *love* Hank."

"I see."

"And you're going to marry Hank," Hank whispered in her ear. Jessie's eyes met his in a melting look. Her happiness was complete at this moment. Nothing else that ever happened in her life would ever outshine this lovely moment. Her bruises would heal, those on her face and those in her heart. She felt utterly loved, utterly loving. Ann was safe, the baby was safe, Hank was here. Everything was wonderful.

"We'll talk when you get home, Bob," she said into the phone. "We have a lot to discuss."

"All right, Jessie."

She slipped the phone back onto the hook and turned fully to Hank's waiting arms. His mouth was gentle on first her bruises and then her lips. "You proposed," she whispered.

"Yes, I did."

"Do you doubt my answer?"

"No."

Her arms squeezed around his waist, knitting their bodies tightly together. "Oh, Hank, I love you so much."

He spoke in a husky, emotion-charged voice. "My sweet, beautiful Jessie. Everything is going to be fine now, isn't it?"

"Yes." Closing her eyes to fully savor the sensation of being in Hank's arms, Jessie felt the stirring of sexual desire, his and hers. She adored this man, and expressing her feelings through physical love was imminently necessary. She stepped back with a soft, "Come with me." Taking his hand, she led him through the house to the staircase.

Hank looked up the stairs then back to Jessie. "We could go to my place."

"Are you uncomfortable here?"

They exchanged a long, meaningful look, and during it, the final shackles of the past fell away. They were quite suddenly only a man and a woman in love. That "wild Farrell boy" and the banker's protected daughter were forever gone.

With a beautiful fluidity, Hank scooped her up into his arms. "Just tell me which room is yours, honey."

Jessie was sleeping, a moonbeam caressing her face. With his pillow bunched beneath his head, Hank looked down at her. Their conversation just before Jessie had drifted off was still alive in his brain.

"Can you forget, Jessie? Maybe I need to know that."

She touched his face. "It's more important to me now that you *forget, Hank."*

"But I don't want you living with that buried inside of you."

Jessie hesitated, then smiled softly. "Let me explain. There's nothing wrong with 'buried.' It's what we both have to do, bury the anger, the frustration, the pain. When I was carrying the burden alone, then it was dangerous. But sharing it with a loved one, being able to talk about it should it surface, weakens its destructive power.

"Darling Hank, neither of us will really forget. My greatest fear was that you would despise me for allowing it to go on for so long. I can only tell you now what I learned from Kelsy. Battered women feel trapped. They become brainwashed, losing any confidence they once had. They're afraid to expose their situation because they're afraid of exposing themselves. And they're constantly afraid of more punishment.

"Hank, some of the damage lasts forever. That's what I must live with, and so, my love, must you. You must guard against bitterness. You must stop hating Allen and hoping for retribution, which would alter nothing. That's what you must realize, that nothing anyone ever does to Allen is going to change what happened to me. I can live with anything but the thought of you becoming embittered and unhappy because of me."

Hank drew a shuddering breath. He couldn't deny that retribution had been in his mind. If any man deserved a punch in the mouth, it was Allen Vaughn.

But Jessie was right. Punching Allen might make *him* feel a little better, but it would change nothing. No, he would never forget, and he knew there would be times when an eruption of outrage might be hard to handle. But they had so much, he and Jessie, and he must concentrate on that.

A small smile relaxed the tension on Hank's face. She still hadn't been up in his helicopter nor had she really inspected the ranch. He still wanted to show off the pups, and the great, ugly rodeo bulls and the Appaloosas. He wanted Jessie and Mick to become friends, so Jessie and Mick's wife could be friends.

Ah, God, life was crazy and unpredictable and... wonderful.

In the moonlight, the bruises on Jessie's face were merely darker shadows and barely visible. She was the sweetest, prettiest little thing he'd ever seen, and he was so full of love for her, it was a wonder his seams weren't bursting.

Sweet on Jessie . . . that's what he was. From the first moment he'd laid eyes on her he'd been sweet on Jessie.

And he always would be.

*   *   *   *   *

Bestselling author **NORA ROBERTS** captures all the
romance, adventure, passion and excitement of Silhouette in
a special miniseries.

THE
CALHOUN WOMEN

Four charming, beautiful and fiercely independent
sisters set out on a search for a missing family
heirloom—an emerald necklace—and each finds
something even more precious...passionate romance.

Look for THE CALHOUN WOMEN miniseries
starting in June.
COURTING CATHERINE
Silhouette Romance #801

July
A MAN FOR AMANDA
Silhouette Desire #649

August
FOR THE LOVE OF LILAH
Silhouette Special Edition #685

September
SUZANNA'S SURRENDER
Silhouette Intimate Moments #397

Silhouette Books®

CALWOM-1

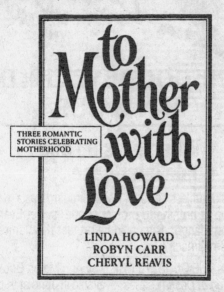

Take 4 bestselling love stories FREE

Plus get a FREE surprise gift!